Aeschylus: Agamemnon

DUCKWORTH COMPANIONS
TO GREEK AND ROMAN TRAGEDY

Series editor: Thomas Harrison

Aeschylus: Agamemnon
Barbara Goward

Euripides: Hippolytus
Sophie Mills

Euripides: Medea
William Allan

Seneca: Phaedra
Roland Mayer

Seneca: Thyestes
P.J. Davis

Sophocles: Ajax
Jon Hesk

Sophocles: Electra
Michael Lloyd

Sophocles: Philoctetes
Hanna M. Roisman

Sophocles: Women of Trachis
Brad Levett

DUCKWORTH COMPANIONS
TO GREEK AND ROMAN TRAGEDY

Aeschylus: Agamemnon

Barbara Goward

Duckworth

First published in 2005 by
Gerald Duckworth & Co. Ltd.
90-93 Cowcross Street, London EC1M 6BF
Tel: 020 7490 7300
Fax: 020 7490 0080
inquiries@duckworth-publishers.co.uk
www.ducknet.co.uk

A catalogue record for this book is available
from the British Library

ISBN 0 7156 3385 6

Typeset by e-type, Liverpool
Printed and bound in Great Britain by
CPI Bath

Contents

Preface   7

Acknowledgements   8

1. Orientation: Aeschylus, Athens and Dramatic
   Poetry   9

2. Theatrical Space   24

3. The Story: Myth and Narrative Technique   43

4. Gods and Humans   69

5. Language, Speech and Silence, Style, Imagery   91

6. The Reception of Agamemnon   109

Notes   131

The Plays of Aeschylus   136

Outline of *Agamemnon*   138

Select Bibliography   144

Chronology   150

Glossary   153

Index   155

Preface

The ancient and appalling history of the House of Atreus, told in different ways, was well-known to the original audience of the *Agamemnon*. Its founder, Tantalus, king of Lydia, was a son of Zeus and favourite of the gods. But he offended them – in some versions by serving up to them the cooked flesh of his own son Pelops as a test of their omniscience – and became one of the four proverbial sinners perpetually tormented in Hades. Pelops himself, his body reconstituted by Demeter, grew up to win a deadly chariot race in Greece against Oenomaus, though not without becoming embroiled in an act of treachery, which resulted in an ineradicable curse. Two of Pelops' sons were Atreus and Thyestes, and in this generation the story becomes one of fraternal rivalry: Thyestes slept with Atreus' wife, Aerope; Atreus expelled Thyestes, then, feigning reconciliation, brought him back for a banquet. In ignorance Thyestes ate the cooked flesh of his own sons before being shown their heads and hands. Expelled again, Thyestes begot an avenger, in many versions by incestuous union with his own daughter. The result was Aegisthus. Atreus himself had two sons, Agamemnon and Menelaus (known as the Atridae), who married two sisters, Clytemnestra and Helen respectively. When Paris abducted Helen, the Greeks mustered a force at Aulis under Agamemnon and sailed away to fight under Troy's walls, leaving Clytemnestra alone. They were away for ten years.

This is the point at which the play begins.

Acknowledgements

I would like to thank the following people: Ruth and Steven Curson and Chris and Ben Goward, who read the manuscript through and made it more lucid. Also, many infelicities (not to say outright howlers) were picked up by Pat Easterling and Susan Woodford, whose encouragement and thoroughly practical advice spring from a rare generosity of nature. Fiona Macintosh was kindness itself. I am very grateful for all this help, and for the support of Tom Harrison and Deborah Blake. Whatever errors remain are indubitably my own.

I would also like to put in a word of thanks to all Greek students at the City Lit, past and present, for the enjoyable and sometimes inspirational discussions resulting from our patient, pooled work on various play texts over the years.

1

Orientation: Aeschylus, Athens and Dramatic Poetry

> There is the sea. And who will drain its resources?
>
> Clytemnestra at 958

Agamemnon is the first play of the *Oresteia*, our only surviving ancient Greek trilogy. Neglected for centuries except as a difficult text for advanced study, over the last hundred and thirty years, the play's treatment of political and familial crisis has inspired many stage productions in fresh translations and adaptations, so that many countries can now testify to its elemental power in performance. Throughout this period of influential and benchmark productions (of both single play and trilogy), scholars have been publishing a wide variety of different critical analyses. Yet, despite so much heavy traffic in both dramatic and academic interpretation, *Agamemnon* still exudes its mysterious aura of unassailable and inexhaustible richness.

The action, however, can be described in a single sentence: 'Agamemnon returns home from Troy in triumph, but his wife Clytemnestra murders him.'

Agamemnon is named after its returning hero, and has a 'return home' or *nostos* story shape. However, the eponymous hero appears only in the central scene (810-974), and his part would not have been assigned to the main actor. The other two plays are named after their female choruses; *Libation-Bearers* (sometimes left untranslated as *Choephoroe*) and *Eumenides*, which means 'The Kindly Ones' and is a way of naming the Furies 'apotropaically', without arousing their powers. In these plays the story continues as follows: 'in revenge, Agamemnon's son Orestes murders Clytemnestra, but is pursued by the Furies for matricide. After receiving purification in Delphi he is at last acquitted by a new court established on the Areopagus in Athens, and the Furies are finally called off by being given a new permanent home there.' The lost satyr play, *Proteus*, which rounded off the trilogy, dealt with Menelaus and Helen in Egypt.[1]

Even when reduced to this scarecrow outline, it is clear that *Agamemnon* lays the ground for a huge design, initiating themes about crime, retribution and justice, and about conflict between male and female and between family (*oikos*) and society (*polis*). These conflicts are repeated again in the second play and finally 'resolved' in the third; in some senses the trilogy shows thesis, antithesis and synthesis. This book sets out to explore some of the brilliant features of *Agamemnon* in its own right: the interplay with contemporary Athens; the range of stunning theatrical effects; the elusive role of the gods in determining human destiny (as embodied in the fates of Agamemnon and Cassandra, and as elucidated by the chorus); the rich and startling language, dense with symbols, personifications and imagery; the play's characteristic mingling of memory and prediction, hope and fear.

Life and times

Aeschylus was born 525/4 BC to a eupatrid or aristocratic family from Eleusis near Athens. He grew up during a period of profound political and cultural development, both of which are reflected in his plays. At the time of his birth, Athens was a kingdom ruled by Peisistratos and his sons. To increase the prestige of their city they had re-organised a local quadrennial festival, the Panatheneia, into a pan-Hellenic event including, besides athletic contests, contests for different kinds of poetry (epic and choral lyric), music and dance. Here the young Aeschylus, whose aristocratic education would anyway have entailed memorising great chunks of Homer and lyric poetry, would had have the opportunity to attend performances by exponents from all over the Greek-speaking world.

Possibly the Peisistratids also re-organised another annual spring festival, the Great Dionysia, establishing for it a contest in tragedy, a new genre of poetry recently developed from choral lyric (this development is described on pp. 18-22 below).[2] Aeschylus probably watched these 'proto-tragedies' too, which, before a theatre was built, would have been performed in the market-place or *agora*. We can only guess at the nature of these early attempts to dramatise myth: Aristotle wrote of 'short plots and ludicrous diction'[3] while Garvie imagines them as 'little more than a messenger speech with lyric content'.[4]

In 510, when Aeschylus was about fifteen, the Peisistratids were expelled and, after a period of turmoil, a democracy was instituted in 508. The first recorded democracy in the world, it was a development springing from the crisis of the times.[5] As Cleisthenes' reforms were gradually implemented, mass citizen assemblies began to meet regularly on the Pnyx to regulate internal affairs and deal with foreign embassies. Mass citizen juries began to determine the fate of litigants in the law courts. Over the next decades these assemblies and juries became a source of civic pride and, if the restructuring of the Great Dionysia to include tragedy took place only now,[6] tragedy would be the third great institution innovated by Athenian democracy.

Aeschylus began to submit tragedies for the festival in *c.* 498, but his first victory (with an unknown entry) was not until 484. Meanwhile Athens was facing a series of threats from Persia. In 490, King Darius had launched an attack, beaten off at Marathon. Both Aeschylus and his brother took part in this battle; his brother was killed. In 480, a second immense invasion began. The Persian navy was defeated at Salamis, largely by Athenian warships manned by citizen oarsmen – though not before Athens itself, abandoned by the civilian population, had been sacked. After the hostile army was seen off at Plataea in the following year, it was possible for Athens to style itself the saviour of the whole of Greece.

We now enter the period of the seven surviving plays (see The Plays of Aeschylus, pp. 136-7 below): *Persians* (472) imagines the outcome of the battle of Salamis from the Persian point of view. It is the only surviving tragedy to take recent events rather than myth as its subject matter (though we know of others in the preceding two decades).

Seven against Thebes is dated to 468-7, but at some point before then, Aeschylus is known to have made the first of at least two trips to Sicily under the patronage of Hieron, the great tyrant of Syracuse and patron of the lyric poets Pindar, Bacchylides and Simonides. On this first visit he probably composed the lost *Women of Etna* to celebrate the founding of Hieron's new city, Etna.

Back in Athens, Sophocles became a fellow-competitor, and defeated Aeschylus with his first entry in 468 (play unknown). By the latest date for Aeschylus' next surviving play *Suppliants* (467-56), Pericles had become a major force in the democracy; in fact, as a wealthy aristocrat, he had funded the production of *Persians* a decade or so earlier. It was with Pericles' backing that the Areopagus court was reformed by Ephialtes and an alliance made with Argos, events reflected and alluded to in *Eumenides*. In 458 Aeschylus won first prize for the *Oresteia*, but not long afterwards returned to Sicily. Perhaps it was there that his Prometheus plays, including *Prometheus Bound*, were performed: there is no external dating, but internal stylistic evidence suggests a date late in his life. The play may have been finished by his son, Euphorion. Aeschylus died at Gela in Sicily in 456/5.

His epitaph, recorded in the unreliable *Life*, refers not at all to his poetry but to his prowess at Marathon. If not composed by his sons, two of whom, in fact, succeeded him as dramatists, the lines might reflect his own deathbed wishes:

This tomb covers the body of the Athenian Aeschylus, son of
  Euphorion.
He died in grain-bearing Gela, but famous Marathon would tell
  of his courage,
And so – with knowledge of it – would the long-haired Persian.

1. Orientation: Aeschylus, Athens and Dramatic Poetry

Aeschylus had experienced a good deal in his lifetime: kings displaced by democrats, and radically new political and legal systems introduced; he had also lived and fought through the equivalent of a World War and faced the threat of imminent slavery; he had seen his city in ruins. He did not live to see the Acropolis, razed in 480 and left derelict in honour to the dead, rebuilt with its splendid Periclean temples, nor the full growth of the Athenian empire. Neither did he see much of the war against Sparta which, within a generation, brought about the decline of the city that could style itself, in the words attributed to Pericles, 'the education of Greece'. The Athenians may have perceived Aeschylus as part of that education. It is said that the Assembly awarded him a unique posthumous honour: tragedies were composed in the first instance for a single performance at the Great Dionysia, but in his case, public funding was provided for further performances (this is not to say that revivals elsewhere did not happen).

The political and social context

The private imagination that created *Agamemnon* reached its public through a thoroughly political filter. The Great Dionysia festival in Athens, where the tragedies were performed, was an opportunity for the democracy to celebrate its achievements. Its administration was entirely under state control. The chief city magistrate (*archon eponymos*) had pre-selected the three tragic playwrights whose works were to be shown. Under the city's 'liturgical' system[7] he had also chosen the citizens who were to finance the choruses. The festival's opening rituals included street processions and sacrifice of bullocks. Then officials took their places in the state theatre and a series of political ceremonies and speeches ensued, including a parade in armour of war-orphans raised at the state's expense. Ten judges, one from each tribe, had already been appointed. The huge citizen audience sat in blocks of seats probably assigned by tribe, with non-Athenians in other designated sections, up to around 14,000 strong in all.[8]

The first contest was for choral song in honour of Dionysus (called dithyramb), held between the ten tribes of Athens, with one chorus of men and one of boys from each tribe, each chorus composed of fifty singers. After the dithyrambic competition came three sets of tragedies, one set performed per day and each set concluded by a satyr play. Satyr plays, with their invariable choruses of satyrs (male hybrids of horse and human) headed by their father Silenos, were, like dithyramb, closely associated with the cult of the festival god Dionysus; their earthy dedication to lust and drunkenness, woven into a mythical plot often connected to the preceding trilogy, alleviated the serious mood. The final competition was between five separate comedies.

Playwright competed against playwright for a single prize, providing an interesting insight into the ideology of equality projected by the democratic *polis*. Athenian society was innately competitive; engaged constantly in war, it also structured its peace-time institutions antagonistically. In the assembly, political debate with speeches for and against was the standard procedure leading to the vote; the law court system too was adversarial. *Agamemnon*, with its scenes of lengthy open debate, its technical legal vocabulary and its general concern with establishing responsibility for wrong-doing and determining punishment, shows a dialectical engagement with the city's democratic processes. The trilogy as a whole famously problematises the nature of justice itself, and is to end in the institution of a civic process which directly mirrors the external city and the recent reforms of its judicial system.

The tragedies themselves, however, contain little public self-congratulation.[9] At this sacred civic festival they are rather, as Nussbaum suggests, vehicles of political reflection, encouraging the audience towards self-examination and change. Emotionally charged, the plays 'challenge the audience to inhabit (the ethical space) actively, as a contested place of moral struggle'.[10] The chorus of male citizens, addressed by Agamemnon as *andres politai*, 'gentlemen of the city' (855) helps the citizen audience identify with their fictional counterparts. Recent experience is mirrored in the play's vivid descriptions of the hardships of campaigning (326-37) and the grief of bereaved families (437-55). The audience too have made the *Oresteia*'s painful move from kingdom to democracy.

The setting of *Agamemnon*, however, is mythical Argos, and Athens itself goes unmentioned. The use of a story remote in time and place enables social norms to be explored and challenged without causing direct offence. One of the norms challenged concerns the role of women, who in contemporary Athens had no political or legal powers and a low social status. They certainly did not act in the plays. Evidence whether women were even permitted to go to the theatre at this date remains inconclusive.[11] In this context, it is remarkable that the most powerful figure of *Agamemnon* is undoubtedly Clytemnestra: this conundrum is considered in chapter four.

The audience is on holiday, but the festival mood created by the initial procedures is solemn; the subject matter of tragedy, like that of epic and choral lyric, is naturally appropriate to the dignified setting. Foreigners ignorant of the tragic genre need to be impressed by this native Attic product. The home audience, meanwhile, have been annually watching plays ever since the revision of the festival programme and, not unlike regular football fans, many are doubtless highly sophisticated spectators, quick to spot stylistic and technical innovations. Each individual probably does his own internal judging, forming opinions on the excellence and weakness of each element – acting, plot construction, dance, singing, language and so forth.

They are in general familiar with the story material Aeschylus uses in *Agamemnon*: the king's disastrous homecoming would be well-known from Homer and other sources. Nonetheless, Aeschylus rivets their attention by setting the myth in a social context they can relate to, by creating novel effects of suspense, and by making them wait for 1,343 verses before the inevitable murder takes place. In the presentation of this story, many effects of irony, suspense and surprise, which seem to us to be the very stuff of theatre, are Aeschylus' own innovations, minted for this festival audience. Such effects were to become almost standard in the hands of later theatre practitioners.

Loss and survival

Before going any further, it is worth emphasising the almost total lack of other contemporary texts, both literary and historical, which would otherwise help in the task of approaching *Agamemnon*. A comparison with Shakespeare is useful here. The vast proportion of his life's output survives, and we are thus able to describe a chronological development and changing themes and techniques. Comparisons with fellow poets and dramatists can be made. Abundant documents can cast light on different aspects, such as contemporary theatres and theatre-managers. Yet even here there are huge areas of uncertainty and debate, such as accurate dating, multiple authorship, adulteration of the text, attribution of speakers and so forth. Even so, to engage in these Shakespearian problems seems a luxury compared to the efforts that must be made with our minimal information about Aeschylus' life and work.

What is more, the surviving texts (dating only from Aeschylus' mid-fifties, after he had been submitting tragedies for at least twenty-five years) come down to us as copies copied many times over, with likely accretions, omissions and errors. Some of these imperfections are evident, others uncertain, others no doubt invisible to us. Despite the painstaking work of scholars, the text of *Agamemnon* is inevitably built on 'decayed and patched foundations'.[12]

Aeschylus was prodigally productive (see The Plays of Aeschylus, pp. 136-7 below). Ninety play titles are attested in the *Suda* (a tenth-century encyclopaedia), seventy in the unreliable *Life*, but of these only seven tragedies survive, and the authorship of the seventh, *Prometheus Bound*, is debated (although in fact normally discussed with the rest of the Aeschylean corpus). It seems that Aeschylus often, but not invariably, produced linked tetralogies, that is four connected plays performed over the course of a single day, three linked tragedies and a satyr play. Certainly *Suppliants*[13] and less certainly *Prometheus Bound*[14] were, like *Agamemnon*, first plays of linked tetralogies. From fragmentary evidence and various attestations we are able to put other play titles together and suggest other tetralogies; ones 'about' Odysseus, Achilles, Ajax and Jason for example, in the sense that this one is 'about' Orestes (whence *'Oresteia'*) are fairly secure. *Persians*, however, was part of a group of plays apparently without a central figure or focus (*Phineus*, *Persians*, *Glaucus of Potniae*, satyr play *Prometheus Pyrcaeus*).

With ten per cent or less of Aeschylus' output surviving, and that only from the last fifteen years of his life, we cannot pretend that we have a representative sample of his work to study. We cannot evaluate the play against the context of his total output, far less against that of his fellow poets. It would be unsafe, for example, to assume that every surmised trilogy of Aeschylus made the same ultimately positive movement from uncertainty and disorder to celebrate human achievement. The fact is, we simply do not have the evidence.[15]

However, in the case of *Agamemnon*, the rest of the trilogy can illuminate at least some of the problems of interpretation. And in a more general way, a good deal of the play's subject matter and treatment, of its formal structure and of its poetic texture, can be understood simply by realising that it is part of a continuing tradition of *poetry*. Attic tragedy is, first and foremost, a synthesis of different kinds of poetry: the great non-Attic genres of epic and lyric, together with the local poetry of the political reformer Solon, archon of Athens 594/3, whose iambic trimeter verse was taken over for the episodes (see below).

Dramatic poetry seems to us qualitatively different from epic and lyric because – obviously – it is performed by actors in a theatre. But the difference between dramatic and earlier poetry is not as great as might be thought. The culture of the archaic and classical periods was a 'performance culture'. There were few written texts. The habit of private reading had barely begun and the term 'literature' had yet to be invented. All types of poetry were heard and seen in performance in settings such as the festivals described above.

Choral lyric

Choral lyric, performed in costume with dance and accompanying music, is tragedy's essential source. The archaic period (660-460) has been described as the great lyric age of Greece and, during this time, any major festival in a community's religious cycle (as well as its victories in battle or at games festivals), was likely to be celebrated by trained choruses performing in a public space. These choruses were composed of representative single-sex groups from the community: men or women, boys or girls as appropriate for the occasion who, elaborately dressed, sang and danced in honour of the god(s) concerned. These costumed choruses, with their music, poetry and dance, were perhaps the most thrilling peace-time spectacle in the ancient world.

Choral lyric was written on commission by professional poets such as Alcman, Stesichorus, Simonides, Bacchylides and Pindar. Though the vast majority of it is lost, sufficient fragments survive to give us a clear idea of the genre. The poems ritually invoke a specific god and/or gods in general, together with hopeful prayers, expressions of fear and anxiety, and general religious and philosophical reflection, often expressed as wise sayings (*gnômai*). As a way of interpreting the relationship between god and man, the poems also tell mythical stories about heroes from myth. A narrative of almost epic length may be related, or a familiar story may receive only a fleeting reference.

Pindar, for example, was a slightly older contemporary of Aeschylus, and his victory odes, composed for winners at the great games festivals in Greece, have survived complete. For the poem *Pythian 4*, Pindar was commissioned to celebrate a victory at the Pythian Games of Arcesilas, king of Cyrene, a North African city originally founded by colonists sailing from the island of Thera. Accordingly, the poem makes a lengthy and flattering analogy between the voyage of the colony's founder and the mythical voyage of Jason and his Argonauts to Colchis. In a high emotional register, Pindar provides a full background to the Argo expedition, details of the voyage, the direct speech of Jason and Medea, and much moral advice.

These characteristics, taken from choral lyric, can be seen in operation in the chorus of *Agamemnon:* the capacity for extensive narration, for moral/religious reflection, and for strong personal emotion. They serve drama wonderfully well: to put it (much too) neatly, the narrative capacity becomes the telling of the play's background story, the religious elements give it intellectual significance, while the emotional tone readily creates suspense and ambiguity about the outcome of the plot.

One member of the chorus had always acted as leader/conductor (the *koryphaios*). Eventually, another member stepped out to impersonate the hero of the myth, using the first person pronoun 'I' rather than the third 'he' to deliver a monologue (which was, perhaps, as Aristotle suggests, initially improvised). This figure would develop into the protagonist of tragedy. When the *koryphaios* began to respond to this 'I' figure also using the first person, we have what to us is the essential situation of drama – a dialogue.

Myth now becomes something that choruses can *enact* as well as *narrate*. 'Thespis' is the elusive figure traditionally credited with adding prologue and speech (as opposed to song) to what had previously been only choral performance, but it is Aeschylus himself to whom the credit belongs for many other innovations. Aristotle's *Poetics* chapter 4, for example, tells us that it was Aeschylus who increased the number of actors from one to two, curtailed the role of the chorus and gave speech the leading part. Aristotle credits Sophocles with being the first to use a third actor, but Aeschylus himself was quick to imitate this innovation, since three actors seem required for *Agamemnon* 782-974 when Agamemnon enters to Clytemnestra with Cassandra behind him on his chariot (it is difficult to see how this could have been otherwise arranged: there seems no unobtrusive moment in the text when a non-speaking actor playing Cassandra could be replaced by a speaking one).

Aeschylus' speed at picking up Sophocles' innovation suggests that tragedy at this time was an innovative form energetically exploring its new medium. In *Agamemnon*, the chorus is still the most significant element, and most scenes consist of only one actor responding to the chorus; at the same time, however, the dilemmas and decisions of individual characters are explored, and a whole range of thrilling dramatic techniques can be seen in place for the first time in recorded theatre history.

Choral origin for drama immediately accounts for many of *Agamemnon*'s features, not least the vast number of lyric verses. Choral odes account for 550 of the play's 1,673 verses; in the episodes, almost exactly half of their remaining 310 verses are also lyric responsions. Their odes are some of the most wide-ranging and philosophically probing passages in the whole of tragedy, but they are still dramatically-evolved descendants of the 'community' lyric from which they sprang and carry out similar functions. Their identity too remains true to their origins. Like all tragic choruses, they are a single-sex group, broadly representative of a particular life-stage, though Aeschylus has added specific idiosyncrasies of characterisation, such as the extremity of their age, and their paradoxical blend of knowledge of the past and blindness to the future.

With its extensiveness and power, the chorus is in a very real sense the backbone of the whole play. The *koryphaios* has much the biggest role of all since, as well as performing the lyrics, in many of the episodes he acts as sole respondent to whichever actor is on stage.

Myth and epic poetry

Another genre of poetry that exerted influence on tragedy was the earliest type of all, epic. Tragedy does not use epic's metre (the hexameter), but its subject matter – myth – is the staple of its story-lines (in fact all ancient poetry of any length uses myth). Most of Aeschylus' surviving plays use myths which had already appeared in Homer or the Epic Cycle (for which see p. 45).

The great forest of myth inhabited by the ancient Greeks is a unique feature of their culture. It is impossible to over-emphasise its influence on all areas of their thought and on all artistic creativity. Recently redefined in a nutshell as 'a socially powerful traditional story',[16] individual myths covered a multitude of subjects: the creation of the universe, the emergence of the Olympian gods, the origins of man, the founding of individual cities, the tales of heroes and their encounters with gods, their feats, adventures, family relationships and deaths. There was no limit on the re-telling and adaptation of such stories. Professional bards, and the rhapsodes who continued their tradition, lived by travelling to festivals round Greece where they gave epic recitations (as did lyric poets too, making use of the same body of material). No doubt these traditional stories were often modified to please local audiences. However, by the beginning of the fifth century, the two great epics of Homer, *Iliad* and *Odyssey*, had come to hold a uniquely influential position in the Greek-speaking world, akin to that of the Bible in the European Middle Ages and Renaissance.[17] To learn Homer as a boy was to receive a moral education: he was thought to teach a man how to live and die courageously, how to relate to his fellow men and to the gods. Homer worked through complex and sophisticated narrative that is by any standard compelling, suspenseful and extremely vivid.

Plato describes Homer as 'first of the tragic poets '(*Republic* 10.607a). The *Iliad* in particular, with its emphasis on loss and suffering, and its evolving focus on inevitable death for Achilles as an individual and for Troy as a community, suggests itself as ready-made for tragedy. The type of discourse it uses is significant too: nearly half the *Iliad* is direct rather than narrated speech, and there is good evidence (e.g. from Plato's *Ion*) that the professional rhapsode, an actor *avant la lettre*, impersonated the characters and acted out their speeches in a highly emotive and dramatic way.

Despite the hierarchical world the heroes inhabit, there is a vast humanity in the poem which encompasses the fates of women and children as well as the warriors; Homer shows immense understanding of psychological motivation, and focuses on human behaviour and reactions in detailed 'scenes', such as the quarrel in council between Agamemnon and Achilles in Book 1, the tender exchange between Hector and Andromache on the wall in Book 6, the encounter at night between Priam and Achilles in Achilles' hut in Book 24, as well as in rarer soliloquies, such as Hector's (22.99-130), his despair wonderfully conveyed in the broken syntax. All this powerful material, 'pre-shaped' for tragedy, was available to Aeschylus. Late evidence that he acknowledged a debt to Homer comes from Athenaeus' *Deipnosophistae* where Aeschylus is attributed with the remark that his tragedies were, 'mere slices from Homer's great banquets'.[18] Some scholars, surveying the vast range of play-titles, have even suggested that Aeschylus had the project of putting the entire epic corpus into tragic form.

The structure of *Agamemnon*
(For unfamiliar terminology see Glossary, pp. 153-4)

By the time *Agamemnon* was performed in 458, tragic poetry – a new and swiftly-evolving form when Aeschylus won his first victory in 484 – had crystallised. A structure had emerged. Plays almost invariably began with a prologue, and then consisted of a basic alternation between choral odes (*stasima*) in a variety of different lyric metres and recited 'episodes' or acts (*epeisodia*), in which up to three actors and sometimes the chorus-leader spoke to each other in iambic trimeters (or, less frequently, tetrameters), tragic poetry's closest approximation to plain prose speech. Another metre, the anapaest, frequently though not exclusively used for entries and exits, was also employed occasionally. These are the three 'levels' of tragic poetry: (1) sung lyric, in a variety of different metrical patterns, each with their own emotional effect, (2) chanted anapaests and (3) recited/spoken trimeters.

1. Orientation: Aeschylus, Athens and Dramatic Poetry

When, within an episode, a stage figure sings and the chorus sing in reply, this is technically called an *amoebaeon* or, if it is a lament, a *kommos*. If one character sings but the other remains speaking in iambic trimeters, this is called an *epirrhematic composition* (in the Cassandra scene, the chorus and the prophetess' fluctuating emotions are brilliantly expressed through their alternations between song and speech).[19] It would be wrong to suggest that tragic structure was at any time rigid: in *Agamemnon* the neat alternation of stasimon and episode breaks down after the fourth episode.

The play is acted by a maximum of three male actors called, in order of importance, the *protagonist, deuteragonist* and *tritagonist*. Female roles were impersonated by men. Pickard-Cambridge suggest that *Agamemnon* requires three actors: the protagonist plays Clytemnestra, 'and the parts of Agamemnon and Cassandra require two further actors (it is only in lines 782-974 that all three actors are on stage together): the parts of the Watchman, the Herald and Aegisthus could be variously assigned to the actors of Agamemnon and Cassandra'.[20] Cassandra is the only role with song, but Clytemnestra has some recitative (1462-1576).

The stage figures wear elaborate costumes and masks which cover their entire face and chin and include a full head of hair. When they sing they are accompanied by an *aulêtês* or double-pipe player.

The Outline of *Agamemnon* on pp. 138-43 has a double purpose. It provides a synopsis of the action while at the same time indicating the play's formal structure, the purpose being to give anyone reading the play in translation some sense of the different constituent types of poetry. Within the episodes the metre is iambic trimeter (unless specified otherwise) and here, if the chorus participates, it will be only the *koryphaios* speaking, not the entire group.[21]

2

Theatrical Space

And now, my dear, step out of that chariot ...
Clytemnestra at 905-6

Imagine you are a director. Holding the script of *Agamemnon* in your hand, walk into the ancient theatre. Actors trail expectantly behind you. Where will you arrange them? What do the different areas of space suggest? How, in short, will you fit the text to the performance space?

This chapter attempts to understand the way the theatre worked when Aeschylus first staged *Agamemnon* in 458, and to describe the theatrical genius with which he exploited it. It tries to describe the experience of watching that first performance, and plots the influence of some of the new special effects in subsequent tragedies.

The physical theatre at the time of Aeschylus

The diagram shows a plan of the ancient theatre in Athens set in context with surrounding buildings. The audience sits in the open air in daylight around the *orchêstra*. Facing them is a *skênê* or stage-building. The *skênê* has a double function. It is a storage place for costumes and masks when the limited number of speaking actors (maximum three) need to change roles, but it also symbolically represents the place where the play is set. Here, the *skênê* represents the palace at Argos, so the orchestra naturally represents the area just outside it. This inside-outside model is in fact used by all subsequent ancient drama, both Greek and Roman, both tragedy and comedy.

In 458 the *skênê* was perhaps a very new invention, maybe no

24

more than ten years old: Aeschylus' three early plays (*Persians, Seven Against Thebes, Suppliants*) seem designed without one. Before the *skênê* came into existence perhaps a small booth stored costumes. The date of its introduction is one of many contested features.

The *skênê* has a door, but the audience cannot see what happens inside, only who comes in and out.

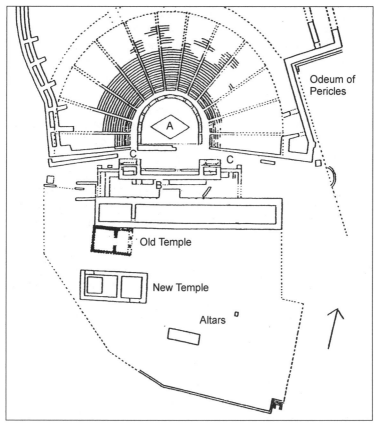

The ancient theatre in Athens. A = *orchêstra*; B = *skênê*; C = *eisodos*. Modified from C*ambridge Ancient History, Plates to vols V and VI* (new edn, 1994), 'The Theatre' by J.R. Green, ch. 7, p. 150.

We need to pause here. The inability to see 'inside' (contrast the effortless movement of the film camera from exterior to interior) is not to be understood as a restriction. It is, in fact, a feature wonderfully exploited by Attic dramatists, who use it to create suspense and to pursue the crisis of knowledge on which so many plots are based. Much of this usage can be traced directly back to *Agamemnon*, the first play to create such a powerful contrast between inside and outside. Aeschylus was probably the first playwright to associate the external *orchêstra* space with what is light, knowable, seeable, rational and (sometimes) masculine, and to contrast it with the internal space inside the *oikos*, which is dark, unknowable, unpredictable and (sometimes) feminine, the place of entrapment and death. This symbolic use of the *skênê* will be discussed further on p. 89 below.

At some point, the inability to show what had taken place inside was surmounted by using a device known as an *ekkyklêma:* a flat cart, which could be wheeled out of the *skênê* with a tableau of actor(s) on it (e.g. Sophocles *Ajax* 348ff.; the device is used satirically by Aristophanes at *Clouds* 184ff.). It must necessarily postdate the *skênê*, since only when an inside has been created does the problem of showing it come into existence. However, even after its invention, events inside still regularly continue to be described first before the display appears. It is not clear if the *ekkyklêma* existed for the *Agamemnon*. When the audience see Clytemnestra and her victims at 1372, it could be that stage-hands brought the bodies out and laid them at her feet.

The two long *eisodoi* or *parodoi* (entrances) are the route by which the twelve members of the chorus enter and leave the theatre; whether it is because they are too numerous to fit into the *skênê*, or because the convention had become thoroughly fixed before the *skênê* evolved, they regularly process into the *orchêstra* after the prologue, singing their entry-song (called *parodos*). Their departure by the same route marks the end of the play; there is no curtain, and the play's entire closing section is known as the *exodos* (departure). Exceptions to conventional practice are always worth considering very care-

2. *Theatrical Space*

fully for their likely 'shocking' effect on the audience, and in *Eumenides* Aeschylus twice uses his chorus of Furies in a startling way: first, they enter (as the text indicates) *fast asleep from the skênê* (could the *ekkyklêma* have been used for this?), and secondly, they leave the *orchêstra* half-way through, to mark the change of setting from Delphi to Athens. Normally the chorus, once on, stay put; when they do leave it is almost invariably to mark a change of place.

By logical convention, actors subsequently entering along an *eisodos* are understood to be arriving from outside the city. Since a fair amount of time elapses between first becoming visible on the exposed *eisodos* and reaching the acoustics of the *orchêstra* to speak, such entries are usually covered by 'entry anapaests', from the chorus, in which they first, perhaps, describe the entrant, and then address him/her. In Aeschylus' hands, this extended entry is exploited to heighten suspense. In *Agamemnon* there are two such entries: first, the Herald, whose unexpected appearance and possible news occupy the chorus for fourteen anapaests (489-502) and secondly, the long-awaited Agamemnon, whose victorious return from Troy is given a sensational fillip by having him enter in a war-chariot, together with Cassandra, his prize of war. The chorus take twenty-seven anapaestic verses (782-809) to chant Agamemnon in.

No gods appear in *Agamemnon* and the gods who come on stage in *Eumenides* enter from along the *eisodoi*, so we do not know whether the *mêchanê* or crane – another device which clearly postdates the *skênê* – had been invented yet. It was later used frequently by Euripides for divine epiphanies (and satirised by Aristophanes, e.g. Socrates' entry, *Clouds* 223ff.).

The actors wear elaborate costumes and masks, and the text of *Agamemnon* indicates that this chorus also carried staves. Mute attendants may accompany the stage-figures: Agamemnon has his soldiers and Clytemnestra her slave-women in the central scene of this play: an actor in such a non-speaking role was called a *kôphon prosôpon*, 'an empty mask'. The *orchêstra* (though possibly containing a natural rock outcrop of some kind) is quite bare and, apart from an altar, to which offerings are often made in the course of a play, there are few stage props. In *Agamemnon*, Cassandra tears off her fillets; in the first half of the next play *Libation-Bearers*, the action is focused around Agamemnon's tomb and the offerings brought to it. Because they are sparse, stage items easily become symbols of great potency, like the 'carpet' in *Agamemnon* (see also, e.g., Hector's sword in Sophocles' *Ajax*, or Orestes' urn in Sophocles' *Electra*).

The use of theatrical space in *Agamemnon*

Such was the space and such the mechanisms for which the text of *Agamemnon* was written. We attempt now to block out possible movements and gestures and, in particular, consider exits and entries which, in the bare ancient theatre, could create great impact. What do we actually see, and what do we understand from what we see? What symbolic dimensions are created?

Taplin's important studies[1] emphasise that Aeschylus was not only a poet. In fact the verb *graphein* (= to write) was not used to describe what ancient playwrights did. The verbs used to describe their activity were *poiein* (= to create, conceptualise, produce), or *didaskein* (= to teach, in the sense of directing the chorus and actors). Ancient playwrights did not write a play for production by others. Early on, at any rate, they realised their own plays themselves in a thoroughly practical way, taking full responsibility for every aspect. They were directors, choreographers and producers for their own work, and probably composed the music and acted one of the roles. Aeschylus composed the text of *Agamemnon* with the physical space of the ancient theatre always in mind.

The full meaning of the work, like the libretto of an opera, is realised only in performance. Our ability to recreate the first performance is hindered by more problems than lack of evidence about the exact nature of the theatre in 458. As with every Attic drama, *Agamemnon* comes down to us with no musical notation, no record of dance movements and no stage directions, so that each exit and entrance has to be inferred from the text. Information from scholia (ancient notes on the text) and hypotheses (ancient summaries of plots) cannot be guaranteed, since it may well reflect Hellenistic productions. Some English translators have not considered these problems, and their invented stage directions can be unlikely. The presence or absence of Clytemnestra on the stage at several points up to 855 is a particularly acute problem, sometimes made worse by the fact that the attribution of speakers can be in doubt. On the subject of Clytemnestra, Taplin convincingly argues that it is not tragic technique to have 'unnoticed flitting to and fro' for any character, let alone such an authoritative one as Clytemnestra: greater authority is established by having her enter at key moments from the *skênê*, speak, and immediately depart. Such incisive movements into and out of the palace better sustain the required sense that it is she who controls the threshold. Modern interpreters in the theatre, however, may make a different choice.

Despite major uncertainties, Aeschylus' brilliant innovation with the theatre space is not in doubt. *Agamemnon* makes bold and powerful use of every single one of its elements, not least its possibly very new *skênê*, to create imaginary dimensions and effects that still shock and frighten.

Agamemnon has a cast of royal characters and a stately chorus. But the first character we see is a common man, watching and waiting on events just as the audience are waiting on the play to unfold. A natural position for a guard looking out for a beacon would be on the roof, and although the text does not confirm this, it seems a very likely position and a natural exploitation of the new *skênê*. The Watchman's magnificent opening sentence (1-7) makes it clear that the *skênê* represents the palace of Argos, a palace which through his prayer is placed at once in relation to the august assemblies and unending movements of the divine powers above it. Then the direction of the Watchman's gaze shifts and, looking along the eastern *eisodos*, he sees the beacon-fire which originated in Troy.

The Watchman's speech thus orientates the audience into

the spatial world of the play. From their seats they 'see' the silent House of Atreus, the space before it, the gods in the cosmos above, and Troy to the East. They will know from which *eisodos* to expect Agamemnon.

The chorus enters (anapaests 40-103), perhaps along the other *eisodos*, which remains spatially unspecific. As their narrative takes us back to the outset of the war, the immediate location fades and we move up again to the circling flight of the eagles and even higher above them (*hupatos*, 55, 'highest') to the indeterminate god who sends a Fury to Troy. Aeschylus then contrasts this free aerial movement with the chorus' earth-bound debility. The chorus, like the setting of the play, is restricted to Argos: ten years ago they were already too old to go to Troy (73-82). Would 'stiff' choreography and sticks reflect their age?

At 84, the present time in Argos returns when they ask Clytemnestra for news. There is debate about her presence here. In Taplin's opinion their request is made through the wall of the *skênê* and she is not visible at this point. At any rate, she makes no reply (the first instance of questions without answers, of problematic communication; an important theme in the play). The vertical axis again dominates their resumed narrative; both in its opening frame, 'persuasion still breathes down upon me from the god' (105-6), and again with the portent of the eagles. Their meditation on the three generations of rulers in Olympus (160ff.) sustains the dimension of height.

The chorus return us to the stage at the end of their *parodos* by saying, 'may it all turn out "as this ever-present sole-guardian bulwark of the land of Argos desires" ' (Denniston and Page's translation of 255-7). But this is another problem. To whom are they referring? Clytemnestra (addressed with some deference in the following iambic trimeters), or themselves? Is the chorus ironically addressing Clytemnestra with the extravagant and deceitful flattery of her own manner, or are they innocently referring to her, at the same time uttering an inadvertent *dysphêmia* (ill-omened expression)? Or could they, despite their extreme age, be referring to themselves as a 'defence'? I emphasise this difficulty to make the point that the problem is not a textual one but one of stage meaning: Aeschylus' direction of the original performance could have removed any ambiguity by the use of gesture.

Clytemnestra's Beacon speech takes us East and upwards again as she lists the series of fire-topped mountains. Inactivity on stage is counter-balanced by the vigour of the urgent leaping flames, as Hephaistus sends them zigzagging westward through space, connecting offstage Troy to onstage Argos. Rosenmeyer well describes a 'growth of excitement and significance'[2] as the description progresses. There is nothing simple or linear about the moving light, which symbolically portends Agamemnon's return from Troy in victory, and which is totally under its narrator's control. Clytemnestra's second narrative returns to Troy and includes a warning. Immediately after delivering it she then makes an incisive exit (350).

The first stasimon opens up and away in Troy. Zeus and Night have thrown a net over Troy's battlements; Zeus' arrow has flown accurately through the air to strike Paris. From 399f., the traffic between Troy and Argos is heavy: *hither* came Paris *from* Troy; *hence* Helen slipped from Menelaus' sight to come *to* Troy. *Hither* now *from* Troy will come the urns bearing the ashes of the dead.

From Troy, an unexpected Herald now arrives. The speech announcing his entry (489-502) is traditionally divided between Clytemnestra (489-500) and the chorus (501-2) but assuming that she exited at 350, the chorus delivers the entire announcement. Their speech not only covers the time it takes the Herald to travel along the eastern *eisodos*, but also creates more tension: he looks auspicious with his olive crown, but can he truly resolve their anxieties?

The Herald makes polar vertical movements, kissing the earth and praying to sun and gods on the rooftops. But the chorus' anxieties multiply. In the Herald's naive account, it becomes clear that the Greeks have indeed offended the gods in their sack: the wreck of Menelaus' ships and his disappearance hint that, somewhere in the eastern distance, on one son of Atreus the gods are already exacting punishment.

The most striking stage action of this scene (if Taplin is right), is the telling moment at which the chorus are recommending the Herald to go in to give the news to Clytemnestra (585-6) – when the doors unexpectedly open to reveal her. Clytemnestra is *dômatôn kuna*, 'the watchdog of the house' (607), and her control over who enters, and when and how, which is established here, will become even more explicit later. After her abrupt appearance, she delivers a single speech (587-614) and disappears again.

In the second stasimon, the chorus yet again visit Troy to consider the effect of Helen's marriage to Paris. But from 750 space becomes indeterminate: their 'old *logos*' about the doom that lies in wait for the generations of the prosperous could apply to onstage Argos as much as to offstage Troy: there is no precise location for *atê* (disaster, 710). Uncertainty is building fast.

Chariot entry

Now the chorus chant anapaests announcing Agamemnon's entry. They hail him, warn of possible unrest among the populace, speak of their own qualms in the past, confirm their own deep loyalty, but hint at the disloyalty of others. All the first part of the play has led up to this moment of return (most recently through the Herald with his repeated *hêkei*, 'he comes' (522, 531). Agamemnon has been repeatedly declared victor of Troy (e.g. 264f., 355f., 524f., 575f.) and light from darkness (25f., 264, 522). But Aeschylus has also made the audience aware of the king's vulnerability to attack from every dimension of the theatre's virtual space: from the gods above, from the populace of Argos (not assigned any spatial dimension), and from persons as yet unspecified within the palace.

Agamemnon enters magnificently on a chariot, though this is not a new departure for tragedy. Cassandra is in the chariot behind him, perhaps hardly visible. Attendants accompany him, probably pulling his chariot, unless real horses were used. We have no indication of how or when the chariot was removed.

Agamemnon's chariot-entry spectacularly symbolises his

triumph over Troy. He reappears after ten years – but only to disappear for good. When he leaves his elevated position to close the scene, it will be to go barefoot and silent into the palace, while his wife speaks. Aeschylus gives Agamemnon a stunning symbolic entry and an equally stunning symbolic exit. Together, entry and exit encapsulate his life's destiny. Aeschylus had used the contrast between a chariot entry and a movement on foot to similar, but less powerful effect in *Persians*. There, the Queen makes an initial chariot entry (*Pers.* 159ff.) but pointedly reappears on foot 'without former luxury' after learning of the defeat (ibid. 607ff.); Aeschylus, with the *skênê* now in place, can recast what is essentially the same feature.

Lure-murder

The greatest and most original *coup de théâtre* is the exact *way* Agamemnon enters the stage-building. The last four lines of his speech (851-4) seem to indicate that he is preparing to go inside of his own accord. Then Clytemnestra, who begins speaking at 855, probably again appears unannounced at the door of the *skênê*, blocking the way (as she did with the Herald at 587). Like Agamemnon, she too has attendants, and at 908 she bids them spread *coverings* (909) to create a *purple-strewn passage* (910). 'Do not ... make my passage grounds for envy by strewing it with *garments*', Agamemnon responds, 'Mortal as I am, it is in no way for me to walk on *beautiful embroidered works* without fear. ... My fame shouts aloud without *foot-wipers* and *embroideries*' (920-7). Later he calls the fabric *sea-workings of the gods* and *wealth, weaving purchased with silver* (946, 949).

These cloths or clothes, over which Clytemnestra and Agamemnon debate, have no mythical precursors. Their use here shows Aeschylus' original and highly developed sense of theatre's symbolic potential: they are surely the most sinister 'prop' in ancient tragedy.

From the abundant and dense language that describes them, what can we understand about their physical appearance? Are they one continuous piece, consisting of several looms-worth stitched together, or a series of separate items of clothing such as cloaks? To think of a carpet is to miss the point. Carpets are made for walking on; Agamemnon's reluctance and the fabric's high value indicate that this is not. The material is *sea-worked* because it has been dyed using a crushed shell (Greek *porphura*, Latin *murex*), a laborious and costly process producing shades in the violet-scarlet range. It has been further worked by embroiderers and so, both in cost and labour, it manifests the wealth of the house (for an excellent discussion, see Jenkins, 1985). The colour is another disquieting aspect: it looks very possibly like blood, although this notion is not developed in this scene.

The crisis of the play approaches. The audience knows that Agamemnon logically cannot remain in his chariot. He must go into the stage-building. But must it be over the 'carpet'? The stichomythia (931-45), with its military language, indicates a verbal battle between husband and wife. The male victor is soon vanquished by the woman's clever words.

The language of 919-25, 935-6 and 946-9 all make it clear that it is dangerous for Agamemnon to walk on the cloth, but what did the action symbolise to the watching audience? They perhaps remembered the 'impious trampling' imagery of the chorus (367ff.), perhaps also Agamemnon's morally dubious earlier actions: the sacrifice of Iphigeneia, the pillage of the army under his command at Troy. Now a *literal* trampling is enacted, which might stand for all his previous morally ambivalent actions. Now too Aeschylus *shows* him in the process of decision, just as before the chorus had *described* him making the decision over Iphigeneia.

At 950 Agamemnon makes the first reference to Cassandra, perhaps only now noticed by the audience in his chariot. The continuous presence of Cassandra established here creates a visual continuity between the two phases of the play (pre- and post-return). A victim from Troy is established in Argos.

The text indicates that, as Clytemnestra begins her speech at 958, Agamemnon begins his walk over the fabric, to disappear inside by the end at 972. Rehearsal must have been necessary to make his walk correspond exactly to the fifteen allotted lines. His movement in this extravagant theatrical exit would be slow. Maid-servants roll up the purple cloths behind him, adding to the sinister sense that this is a one-way-only journey. It matters that Clytemnestra's voice dominates his silent walk. Finally, after 974, husband and wife are to be imagined together inside the palace, privately re-united for the first time in ten years.

If the *skênê* was indeed a recent invention, Aeschylus had lost no time in exploiting it to the full in this splendid exit. He makes use of the same scene-type in his next play, *Libation-Bearers*. This time it is Aegisthus who is lured inside to his death. In a previous scene Orestes, by entering in disguise and announcing his own death, has managed to gain access to the palace (Clytemnestra's control over the threshold has slipped). He waits inside while Aegisthus is enticed in 'to hear the news' by Orestes' old Nurse, who has been primed for the purpose. As Orestes (in the audience's imagination) exacts his revenge inside, the chorus is left alone onstage to reflect the tension (841ff.). After the murder a tableau follows, showing Orestes standing over his kinsman's corpse.

Similarly-constructed scenes, in which the murder victim is tricked or lured inside, leaving the chorus to chant or sing, 'covering' the invisible murder on the empty stage, may be found in Sophocles' *Electra* and in Euripides' *Medea*, *Hecuba*, *Heracles*, *Electra* and *Orestes*. A horrible irony is created in each case: the audience watch the ignorant victim duped and disappearing. They know that he/she will not reappear alive, and that theatre convention debars intervention from the omnipresent chorus. As helpless as them, the audience can only wait to hear the cries from within.[3]

In the following stasimon the chorus is deeply disturbed – and disturbed by its own disturbance. They cannot understand why terrible anxiety should be their reaction to witnessing the reunion of their victorious king and his wife. It is surely puzzlement (rather than full realisation) that Aeschylus wished to inspire in his original audience by the action of the previous scene. Agamemnon's exit looked like a kind of trap and clearly had sinister significance, but its exact import (like that of all effective symbols and symbolic actions, in fact) surely continues to remain enigmatic: the audience will understand its meaning more fully only after another doomed exit into the house – Cassandra's (1330). Meanwhile, in this stasimon the irrevocability of Agamemnon's exit seems to emerge almost unheeded at 1019ff., where the chorus ponder, 'who by an incantation could summon back dark blood, once it has fatally fallen before a man?' Here *propar andros* ('before a man, at a man's feet') suddenly seems to refer to the walk on the purple cloth.

After this lyric, the audience logically expects Agamemnon's murder to follow; though an onstage presence, Cassandra has been given little significance as yet. At 1035 it is a surprise when Clytemnestra re-enters and we realise the situation inside the palace is as yet unchanged. The following scene is an intriguing meeting of wife and mistress, two women with opposite and exceptional powers over language – the weapon of one is eloquence, the other, unbroken silence.

With the same veiled intent and using the same phrase as for her husband, *ekbain' apênês têsde*, 'get down from this chariot' (906, 1039), Clytemnestra attempts to get Cassandra into the house. This time, however, she cannot initiate a dialogue. Cassandra's persistent silence implicitly contrasts with that of Agamemnon. Having previously 'won', we now see Clytemnestra defeated by the prophetess' lack of response; this is the first time we have seen her eloquence defeated.

Silence and the kôphon prosôpon

The sustained power of Cassandra's fascinating silence must make the audience now realise that she is too important to be a mere *kôphon prosôpon*, a non-speaking actor. Having thus created intense audience interest in a figure characterised by *silence*, Aeschylus transfixes them by her extraordinary *utterance*. So far, within the episodes no character has sung, and so her song here is in itself a new element. But that is not all. The moment when she opens her mouth is a *coup de théâtre* and begins a significant alteration in the prevailing character and direction of the play. Aeschylus gives his prophetess a new, frenzied, extraordinarily arresting and individual voice, and in the course of her scene (1071-1330), the virtual space of the play undergoes a radical shift.

Earlier on, we said there was a convention of having non-speaking actors on the stage (*kôpha prosôpa*), often to create a sense of status – companions, members of a retinue, etc. Aeschylus here cleverly makes his audience at first think that Cassandra is one such *kôphon prosôpon*. In *Libation-Bearers* he pulls the same trick to even greater effect: Pylades is Orestes' conventional companion, and silently accompanies him throughout the play until the critical moment of matricide arrives. Then Clytemnestra bares her breast and dares Orestes to kill her, his own mother. As Knox describes it, 'And Orestes breaks. The command of the god Apollo, the unavenged blood of Agamemnon murdered in the bath, Orestes' own exile and poverty, all the forces behind him – gods, family and his own ambition – fail him at this supreme moment. He turns to the silent figure who has followed him step by step throughout the play and asks him a direct question: "Pylades, what am I to do?" And now at last Pylades speaks. He has only three lines but they are enough: "Then what becomes in the future of Apollo's oracles, what meaning in the sworn pledge of faith? Better offend the whole human race than the gods." It is the voice of Apollo himself; these three lines seal Clytemnestra's death warrant. ... The third actor in *Libation-Bearers* is used to dominate the stage for one tremendous moment in which mother and son hang on his words for life or death.'[4]

Aeschylus was famous for his silent figures, who are satirised by Aristophanes at *Frogs* 911-13; we know that a muffled, silent Achilles began two of the three plays of his lost *Achilleia* trilogy. The silent presence of children at the end of Sophocles' *Oedipus Tyrannus*, and Deianeira's shifting sense of Iole's silent identity among the captive women in Sophocles' *Trachiniae* testify to the eerie power of stage silence – of which Aeschylus was the originator.

In *Agamemnon*, the significance of Troy, so important earlier, now fades and is relevant only to Cassandra's past life. At last the physical identity of the *skênê* comes to the fore and with it, the long-disguised significance of the house facing the audience. We have reached the play's core: the past, present and future destiny of the House of Atreus.

Oikos (house) in Greek designates both physical building and abstract sense of *household*, the sum of family members. It also means 'ruling house', and substance of the house, in the sense of its total wealth of land and material possessions, not least including its offspring. The continuity of the house in the begetting of children and in careful economic management is central to Greek thought and stressed in many texts. *Oikos* can also contrast with *polis*, as personal contrasts with political. Further, *oikos* can mean *inheritance*, a meaning which illuminates the chorus' notion of a doom passing down the generations.[5]

This is the House of which the Watchman said that, if it could find a voice, it would speak most clearly (37-8). Soon it *will* find a terrible voice, virtually at least, as Agamemnon's death-cries resonate from within (1343, 1345). Meanwhile, we have seen that Clytemnestra controls its threshold and that she made her husband trample on its substance. Clytemnestra argued that 'the house doesn't know poverty' (962); but already the chorus have pointed to the vulnerability of prosperity (750f.). All the action of the play so far has led into this house. Under Clytemnestra's control, the Herald entered, Agamemnon has entered, and Cassandra too must finally go inside.

Cassandra's function in this scene is to reveal the house's hidden horrors. As soon as her shrieks become comprehensible, she asks what *house* Apollo has led her to, and the chorus emphatically confirms it to be *the House of Atreus* (1087-8). The audience consider afresh the *skênê* in front of them, which Cassandra immediately describes as *misotheon* (an adjective inextricably meaning both 'hated by' and 'hating' the gods); a house that is 'well aware of kin-murder ... (next word corrupt) ... a human slaughter-house and blood-spattered ground' (1092). In it are the slaughtered weeping babies and their roast flesh, which their father ate, and in the bathhouse a new terrible evil: '(Clytemnestra) stretching out hand after hand, reaching them out' (1110-1). 'What Fury are you summoning to raise its cry through the *house*?' ask the chorus (1119).

The house remains dominant when Cassandra tries again to communicate her visions in iambic trimeters. 'A chorus that chants in unison, but is not melodious, never leaves this *house* ... Look! A revelling band of Furies of the family waits in the *house*, hard to send out, drunk on human blood to give itself greater boldness. Sitting in siege on the *house* they sing of primal *atê* ... (1186ff.). Again at 1214ff., she asks the chorus to '*see* the children, like figures in dreams, their hands imploringly holding their own flesh, assailing this *house* ... they are utterly clear'. As the scene approaches its end, the text indicates that three times Cassandra goes up to its door, bravely walking into her own destruction (1291, 1306, 1313). Addressing it as the 'gates of Hades' now has a real and powerful meaning. She is repelled by the house's smell of blood, 'the vapour that comes from a tomb', but finally enters, speaking magnificent lines on the human condition as she does so. The autonomous dignity of her exit makes an ironic contrast to Agamemnon's silent withdrawal.

The chorus begins to reflect on what they have just witnessed, but their understanding is still dawning when there is a shock: Agamemnon's death-cries heard through the wall of the stage-building (1343 and 1345; the chorus begins its reaction on 1344). We have, perhaps, been expecting these cries ever since Agamemnon's exit at 974, but the powerful interest of the long Cassandra scene has diverted our attention, so Aeschylus brings it about that the king's cries fall on our ears with a painfully renewed sense of the inevitable.

Offstage cries

This is the first known example of an offstage voice being projected through the wall of the *skênê*, and another new theatrical technique to be attributed to Aeschylus. The main effect, of course, is to make the murder palpably immediate to the audience. At *Libation-Bearers* 869, Aegisthus similarly cries through the wall.

Sophocles and Euripides further developed this feature of offstage cries in lure-murders, always to the end of making a murder seem more real. At Euripides *Medea* 1271ff., the little boys cry out offstage (in iambic trimeters), and the chorus reply in dochmiacs, picking up their vocabulary. The close verbal interaction makes their lack of physical intervention particularly horrible. In other plays, when a stage figure remains on stage as well as the chorus (as for example, at Sophocles *Electra* 1398ff., Euripides *Orestes* 1246ff.), a vivid chain of communication can be created, as the one nearer the *skênê* can give a blow-by-blow account of 'what they hear' to the other. Sometimes even further immediacy is created when a line or lines of verse are divided between speakers on either side of the *skênê* wall, as when Electra eggs on her (offstage) brother to kill Clytemnestra (Sophocles *Electra* 1410ff.; such a divided line is called *antilabê*). None of these effects, of course, could take place before the *skênê* evolved.

Offstage voices, whether only imagined or actually heard by the audience, went on to be quite commonly used outside the context of a lure-murder. There are, for example, two instances in Euripides' *Hippolytus* which both create a tremendous immediacy: first, at 565ff., in a scene charged with horror and tension, Phaedra, with her ear to the wall, gives a blow-by-blow report to the chorus of 'Hippolytus' reactions to the Nurse'; later in the play at 776, the offstage Nurse cries out for help (this time audibly) – Phaedra has just hanged herself.

The cries are heard, and from 1346-1371, Aeschylus capitalises wonderfully on the chorus' conventional inability to 'go inside'. Instead, they break down into their constituent members, and in the twelve two-line speeches of this section, an array of contradictory suggestions and proposals are made to meet the crisis. We can only imagine the chorus' movement at this point – certainly a vivid onstage portrayal of political chaos is created. Before they are anywhere near deciding how to respond, Aeschylus introduces his next shock: Clytemnestra appears.

Tableaux

If early tragedy, as is likely, contained a great deal of message narrative, the original audience might well have expected a messenger to emerge at this point. A servant could easily fill this role (as at *Libation-Bearers* 875f.) They are perhaps startled to see Clytemnestra herself appear so quickly from the door of the stage building – yet she has done so already four times previously (258, 587, 855, 1035). All these entries were theatrically powerful, but none more so than this fifth one in which her naked power is finally revealed. Holding a weapon, she stands over the corpse of Agamemnon, wrapped in a net, and that of Cassandra. Whether positioned on an *ekkyklêma* or not, the tableau visibly represents the fulfilment of the play's action. Words are temporarily redundant.

There is a mirror tableau in the next play when Orestes appears triumphant over the body of his mother. By using an identical tableau, Aeschylus gives the audience visual evidence that the successive murders are both reciprocal and identical; they understand that the House of Atreus is doomed to repeat its bloody acts.

Tableaux are found in subsequent plays and do not always display corpses – there are, for example the sleeping Furies in *Eumenides* and the grotesque sight of Ajax sitting on a heap of slaughtered animals in Sophocles *Ajax*. Their effect is always to make the audience gasp.

In the *agôn* which follows Clytemnestra's speech of triumph, as she and the chorus attempt to establish the real responsibility for the crime, the visual focus stays on the figures from the tableau – the murderess and her major victim. But other dimensions are activated as well: the House is falling under a hail of blood (1532ff.); Hades below is Agamemnon's destination (1528f.), where Iphigeneia will welcome him (1555f.).

Eventually both chorus and Clytemnestra come to agree that

the *daimôn* or *alastôr* (spirit or avenging spirit) of the House was active in the murder, and at this point the tragedy seems about to end, in an uneasy compromise. Aeschylus now gives us his final surprise entry: Aegisthus, with henchmen. He enters from outside (see 1608), perhaps symbolising his return from exile and showing clearly that he has played no active part in his cousin's murder. Clytemnestra's verses 1567-1576 would be delivered as he becomes visible, but there is no usual entry-announcement; perhaps he slinks in. His final exit, however, is into the palace with Clytemnestra – a life's ambition visibly achieved and a marked contrast to Agamemnon's earlier 'defeated' exit.

Aegisthus gives a lucid account of Thyestes' banquet (1583-1602). From a new standpoint he fully confirms the accursed (1602) history of the House, previously described in Cassandra's visionary glimpses and thrashed out by Clytemnestra and the chorus. His naked power is brutal and almost provokes a stage fight (1650-1); sufficiently so, at any rate, to demonstrate that the chorus is too weak to resist. Though they invoke the *daimôn* to bring Orestes back for revenge, Clytemnestra persuades them to leave. The text of the ending is defective, but Aeschylus does not seem to have written the usual exit anapaests for them. Is this another innovation, to make their departure piece-meal and disjointed, in accordance with their diminished status? As the play ends, Clytemnestra and Aegisthus go into the palace to begin their new, oppressive regime.

3

The Story: Myth and Narrative Technique

I'd like to hear your story again and admire it from beginning
to end ...

Chorus to Clytemnestra, 318-19

This chapter turns away from Aeschylus' wizardry in the theatre
to refocus on his genius as a story-teller. To get a perspective on
his narrative strategies, we shall first survey earlier versions of
the myth of Agamemnon's murder, and then discuss in some
detail the way Aeschylus re-worked it for the stage.

Literary precursors: earlier treatments of the myth

The Trojan War background of *Agamemnon* comes essentially
from the *Iliad*, with some interesting differences of detail. In
Homer, Agamemnon has a son, Orestes, and three daughters,
Chrysothemis, Laodice and Iphianassa; no Iphigeneia as such
(and no Electra). In the opening book, Agamemnon remarks
that he prefers his concubine Chryseis to his wife (*Iliad* 1.113-
15; at *Ag.* 1439 Clytemnestra seems to echo this when she refers
to Cassandra as 'a Chryseis'). Aulis is the muster point for the
outgoing ships and the place where a significant portent
occurred which received interpretation from Calchas (2.299-
330), but there is no adverse wind, nor daughter-sacrifice. On
the Trojan side, Cassandra is cast as merely one of Priam's
daughters with no prophetic powers. She is briefly mentioned
only twice: her betrothed dies in battle (13.361ff.); she is the

first to see Priam's return from the Greek camp (24.697-701). The context seems to indicate keen eyesight, not foresight.

The *Odyssey* is the major source for *Agamemnon*. In fact it contains a bewildering variety of accounts of Agamemnon's return and murder, and of the revenge taken by his son. The divergency of these accounts, with their different details and emphases, are best accounted for as varying according to the speaker – his point of view within the text, and his persuasive intention towards his listener. The level of Clytemnestra's participation in her husband's murder varies considerably.

In the *Odyssey*, the triad of husband, wife and son (Odysseus, Penelope and Telemachus) are frequently compared with the triad of Agamemnon, Clytemnestra and Orestes to create an alternative narrative model.[1] In Books 1-4 (the *Telemachy*), there is a concern to rouse the young Telemachus into action on behalf of his wronged father, and Orestes is brought in to be a positive role model for this purpose. Athena, Nestor and Menelaus (quoting Proteus) all narrate what looks like a plain tale of male revenge in which Clytemnestra's role is insignificant: Aegisthus is the sole villain in all these accounts. He commits adultery with Clytemnestra and murders Agamemnon on his return at a feast. Agamemnon dies 'like an ox at the stall' (4.535, repeated 11.411). In revenge, Orestes rightly murders him: the killing marks the satisfactory end of the story.

Homer creates no sense of a generational conflict. Thyestes' name is mentioned, but there is no mention of the strife of the previous generation (known to us from other sources), when the wife of Atreus was seduced by Aegisthus' father Thyestes, and in return Atreus perpetrated an horrific revenge at a banquet, at which in ignorance Thyestes ate his own murdered children.

In the second half of the *Odyssey*, two scenes in the underworld make more of Clytemnestra's role and bring us closer to Aeschylus' own plot-line: when Odysseus visits Hades, Agamemnon's shade tells him that Aegisthus and his own wife both contributed to his murder; Clytemnestra personally killed

Cassandra in the same coup: Clytemnestra's bigger role here can be seen as motivated by Homer's need to have Agamemnon make a negative comparison between his own faithless wife and Odysseus' loyal Penelope.

While in the Underworld, Odysseus makes a comment which for the first time in Homer's poem seems to predicate the exact story-line of *Agamemnon*:

> Alas, right from the start, how much all-seeing Zeus has been a relentless foe to the House of Atreus, working his will through women's counsels. It was for Helen's sake that so many of us died, and it was Clytemnestra who hatched the plot against you her absent lord.
>
> *Odyssey* 11.436-9; for a similar idea see also 24.24-9

It is all here: a generational saga in which the House of Atreus figures in a problematic relationship to Zeus. And in fact the chorus' words at *Ag.* 1453ff., as they juxtapose the deadly effect of the two sisters, seem a reverse echo of Odysseus' second remark:

> By a woman's hand (i.e. Clytemnestra) he perished. Alas, frenzied Helen, how very many lives you destroyed under the walls of Troy ...

Treatments of the story after Homer and before Aeschylus, which survive only in a fragmentary form, show developments in the already fluid story-patterns found in the *Odyssey*. The Epic Cycle was a series of post-Homeric poems that formed a vast sequence covering the entire heroic age. Six of them appeared to fit round the Homeric poems to create an enormous cycle including events before, during and after the Trojan War which Homer himself did not relate. The poems themselves (inferior in quality to Homer's) survive only in tiny fragments, but in the fifth century AD they were summarised in prose by Proclus, and fragments of this work have survived.[2] His epitome of one poem, the *Cypria*, which was a 'prequel' to the *Iliad*, provides the earliest source for the information that Iphigeneia faced sacrifice at Aulis. This sacrifice was brought about by the need to conciliate Artemis, who had been angered by Agamemnon's boast that he surpassed the goddess in archery. However, at the last minute the goddess substituted a deer and the girl was saved (as in the story of Abraham and Isaac). This appears to have been the more canonical version of the story – certainly it is the one Sophocles uses in *Electra* and Euripides in *Iphigeneia in Tauris* and *Iphigeneia at Aulis* – and raises the question whether Aeschylus then made a bold innovation in having Iphigeneia *actually* sacrificed.

In the *Cypria* the figure of Cassandra has developed too: for the first time she is as she appears in *Agamemnon:* a prophetess foretelling the doom of Troy, and Agamemnon's prize.

In the later archaic period, lyric poets seem to have promoted Clytemnestra to either joint participant or primary instigator in Agamemnon's murder. Tiny surviving fragments from Stesichorus' two-book lyric *Oresteia* suggest this, and Pindar's epinician ode, *Pythian XI*,[3] glancingly treats Clytemnestra as the *only* murderer, asking the question whether her motive was anger at Iphigenia's death or passion for Aegisthus. A beautiful but baffling painting on the Boston krater, dated to approximately 470 BC, shows Agamemnon enveloped in a diaphanous net: Aegisthus kills him with a sword, while Clytemnestra follows up with a double axe. March[4] suggests that this painting might have been inspired by a now lost poem (possibly by Simonides) treating the story along these lines. Note the two murder weapons on the vase. It is interesting that Clytemnestra's weapon in *Agamemnon* seems to vary: at 1262 and 1528 a sword is implied; but at 1149 and 1520 the weapon is an axe.

As to the site of the murder, we do not know who originated the shift from banquet to bath, but since the bath was the place where, in epic tradition, women on their own attended naked and vulnerable men after their travels, the altered location is exactly right for a female murderer.

Drawing what conclusions one can from the scant evidence,

it seems that by the time Aeschylus came to compose *Agamemnon*, he had a variety of sources to choose from. The story was clearly well known in various versions, but later ones had increased Clytemnestra's involvement in her husband's murder. Either Aeschylus himself or an earlier lost source had given her much greater motivation by having Agamemnon sacrifice their daughter.

Whatever the precedents, however, story tradition was always fluid, and it would be a mistake to think that Aeschylus was in any way obliged to follow the most recent casting of the story. As a creative poet he was bound to the basic outline, but not restricted to the detail of any previous version. Furthermore, because he was dramatising it, he needed to find new ways of treating narrated story material to make it work for the stage. A similar analogy would be the strategy needed by a script-writer to adapt a novel for cinema or television. It may be that Aeschylus was the first dramatic poet to realise the need for, and fully effect, this different strategy, and the brooding physical presence of the House, the symbolic walk along the carpet, the visionary horrors of Cassandra must all spring from the realisation that the audience can be powerfully affected by what it *sees* as well as what it hears. Aeschylus was the first poet to dramatise this story, and *Agamemnon* is testament to his genius at transforming epic narrative into dramatic art.

Suspense

If Aeschylus had followed the almost invariable technique of Euripides, an opening prologue-speaker delivering a programmatic speech would have outlined which particular story-line his play was adopting and – given the extensive history of the House of Atreus over many generations – where it would end (the *telos* or *terma*). The clear exposition of *Hippolytus'* prologue speech makes an ideal comparison. Aeschylus' narrative strategy works in exactly the *opposite* way and he deliberately does neither of these things: his purpose thereby is to create suspense.

Suspense has been variously defined. One usefully simple definition is 'an emotion ... arising from a partial and anxious uncertainty about the progression or outcome of an action'.[5] Chapter 1 outlined the play's action: 'Agamemnon comes home from Troy victorious, but his wife Clytemnestra kills him.' That is the 'story' of the play, an abstraction, giving the events in chronological sequence. As the audience waited for the play to begin, they undoubtedly knew this story. How then can suspense be aroused?

Theoretical models, sophisticated enough to account for the complex ways audiences respond, can supply some insights into the way this works. The 'audience morphology' of Rabinowitz[6] makes a distinction between an *authorial* and a *narrative* audience. The authorial audience consists of people with a similar historical and cultural background to the author himself. They are thus capable of responding to new elements in a story or to any contemporary allusion, as well as being able to evaluate the work objectively as it unfolds (what we might call the 'sophisticated' audience). The members of the narrative audience, on the other hand, are in a liminal state, their own lives temporarily arrested as they give their attention to the action before them. This audience temporarily assents to forget what it knows, responding on a minute-by-minute basis to the unfolding action, and allowing itself to be unaware of the outcome ('naïve' is not the right word to describe this essential engagement).

Rabinowitz's model is of course theoretical only, since real individuals react simultaneously in both ways. It is not uncommon to feel objective admiration for a fine performance while at the same time being involved enough in the drama to be physiologically affected by it, to the level of altered breathing and accelerated heart-rate. The value of the model is in providing a basis for the disturbing and often contradictory range of effects Aeschylus can arouse, as his audience shifts uncomfortably from an external to an internal view of events on stage, from a largely intellectual to a largely emotional response.

3. The Story: Myth and Narrative Technique

The model also makes it clear that within each member of the audience discrepant levels of awareness are in operation: they both know and do not know. And Aeschylus makes discrepant awareness, different levels of knowledge, a key part of his strategy to arouse suspense. In this play discrepant awareness operates at every level, between audience and stage-figures, and between individual stage figures. With their knowledge external to the play, the audience knows more than the chorus. Yet Clytemnestra knows more about the future than both the chorus *and* the audience: only Cassandra knows more than Clytemnestra: ironically, this will not save her life. Discrepant awareness creates rich audience involvement, and all the abundant varieties of dramatic irony, seen perhaps most prominently in the exchanges between Cassandra and the chorus, where irony is by turns grim, grotesque, pathetic, even momentarily funny.

A different model, this time directed towards the story, can also aid our understanding of suspense. Russian Formalists in the early twentieth century initiated a distinction between story and plot (subsequently reformulated in various different ways by structuralists and post-structuralists). 'Story' consists of the basic story material arranged as a sequential chain of events (e.g. the action described at the beginning of the first chapter of this book), whereas 'plot' is the particular ordering and presentation of these events constructed by a specific author, which may be very differently cast. They argued that the divergence between these two elements of story and plot, in the experience of reading or watching, created an essential effect of 'defamiliarisation', by means of which familiar material became strange and suspenseful again.

The audience knows in outline the outcome of Agamemnon's return (the *'what'* of the story), but they do not the *'how'* of the plot: they do not know which (if any) particular version Aeschylus is adopting. And Aeschylus deliberately creates a plot full of subterfuge (via the chorus and his heroine), one in which the chronological sequence of past events – the only key to the causality of the murder – is wildly obscured and disordered. His audience is thoroughly 'defamiliarised' and kept in a state of uncertainty to the highest degree and for as long as possible.

Aeschylus planned the three plays of the *Oresteia* to have a massive temporal span, extending from the mythical fall of Troy and the return of Agamemnon, through Orestes' matricide and pursuit by the Furies to the historical establishment of the court of the Areopagus. The most obvious connective thread between the plays is revenge and reversal, and the resolution of the conflicting claims to Justice (*Dikê*). But it is typical of his narrative strategy not to reveal any of this at the outset, and to begin instead with an ignorant, expendable figure whose sole function is completed at 1.22, once he has seen the signal fires. Yet the fires indicate victory and Agamemnon's imminent return, and so the play gets under way. In the following scenes this return becomes gradually nearer and more real: the signal fires described by Clytemnestra become the specific geography of the Beacons; her words also re-create the fallen city; then the Herald gives his independent eyewitness report of Troy's fall. Then Agamemnon himself returns.

But the slow forward movement is more complex than this. Each scene in fact has a similar shaping: good news arrives, bringing Agamemnon nearer; but the positive forward movement is always followed by negative suggestion;[7] layers of discrepant awareness develop, gaps about the past and fresh uncertainties about the future emerge, and by the end of the scene there is as much to fear as to hope for. But the stage figures do not reveal exactly what they fear so much. Meanwhile there is a thematic unravelling of any certainty achieved, which we see when the chorus express their confidence in Clytemnestra's report at 351f. only to fall prey to uncertainty again at 475f.. All the characters are reluctant to give a full account of what they know; they merely warn or hint, then refuse to speak and fall silent. The Watchman begins this process (36-7):

As for the rest, I'm silent. Big ox on my tongue.

Similarly, Aeschylus created a Herald (not present in traditional accounts) who first of all confirms the fall of Troy with his eyewitness account, but then inadvertently confirms that the feared desecration of holy places at Troy has occurred. Only when prodded by the chorus does he reluctantly reveal more bad news – the shipwreck of the returning fleet and the disappearance of Menelaus. We may believe, though no character articulates the thought (least of all the Herald himself), that the gods are already exacting punishment.

In these opening scenes Aeschylus seems concerned to thematise the human experience of waiting in suspense, with all its emotional baggage – hopes and fears supported by a wealth of unsupported and contradictory conjectures. We have to remember how well-known the story was, and therefore the boldness of this strategy of enforcing a return to complete ignorance.

Aeschylus had made an even more startling, almost perverse, use of the same technique fourteen years earlier in his historical play *Persians*, where, by shifting the setting to the Persian court, the outcome of the battle of Salamis could similarly become the object of intense expectation. 'Waiting for a hero's return' is part of *nostos*-structure (a plot centred round homecoming), and the focus on those waiting ultimately derives from the second half of the *Odyssey*, but its development in tragedy is due to Aeschylus. *Libation-Bearers* too begins with waiting (Electra waiting for Orestes), and Sophocles and Euripides imitated this shaping in their own Electra plays. It also occurs in Sophocles' *Trachiniae* and in several Euripidean plays opening with suppliants desperately awaiting a rescuer (e.g. *Heracles*, *Andromache* and *Supplices*). Aeschylus' strategy here, as in so many other areas, influenced the shaping of many subsequent tragedies.

Time

Aeschylus' stage figures as they wait are enmeshed in the passage of time. Another of Aeschylus' suspense-arousing strategies is to disturb the natural sequence of events in time, opening gaps and creating that sense of defamiliarisation. As described elsewhere,[8] Aeschylus uses the chorus to set up a kind of narrative pendulum which sweeps over the 'now' of the present without stopping: instead we receive tantalising accounts from different, unconnected points in the past. As the mighty lyrics of the chorus keep returning us to the past, we realise that it is only by understanding it that the future could ever be predicted. Yet we are disabled by the chorus' self-censorship and incomprehension. Manifestly, some things are too painful for them to admit, or too well known to mention (1106); in fact they have a variety of excuses. Ultimately, their knowledge of the past, wide-ranging though it is, fails to predict, far less prevent, the murder.

From the moment the Watchman sees the beacon, the *telos* or goal of the action is set to be Agamemnon's return, and that simple return seems to define the temporal extent of the play. But the chorus then takes us back ten years to the setting out from Aulis (40ff.) and, within that account, right back to the earliest time of all, the creation of the world by Ouranos and Gaia (160ff.). We are returned to the recent past when Clytemnestra describes the passage of the Beacon fires and speaks of the previous night's events in Troy (281ff., 320ff.): the chorus' next ode begins with the same recent time as it contemplates Troy's fall (351ff.), but soon becomes a timeless moral reflection before settling on yet another earlier past time, when Paris seduced Helen and she came to Troy (399ff.). Now the Herald speaks of more immediately recent events: the victory (524ff., 551ff.) and the wreck of Menelaus' fleet (636ff.): this only spurs the chorus to go back yet further to an earlier point in time, to consider the figure who named Helen at her birth (681ff.). Even after Agamemnon enters, Clytemnestra insists on telling him at length about her ten years of waiting (855ff.).

The great Cassandra scene in itself has an extraordinary temporal relationship to the present time of the play, seeming to take place in 'arrested' rather than real time – between

Clytemnestra's exit at 1068 and Agamemnon's death cries at 1343. Its final effect is to distract us from the forthcoming murder so successfully that when the death-cries are eventually heard they come as a surprise after all.

The Cassandra scene has no 'real' present time but in it new narratives from the past and future are at last offered, and into the consciousness of the play for the first time comes the awareness that the real *telos* is not Agamemnon's *return* but his *murder* on his return. The new narrative fragments, delivered in a context of raw pain and frenzied emotion, alter the audience's vision. Aulis and Troy as narrative *loci* fade away, and the past now concerns the history of the physically present House of Atreus: we have at last reached the true epicentre where the *telos* is to be played out; for the first time we begin to understand that this *telos* is the most recent link in a chain of Atreid events all played out exactly *here*. It began with the primal and original disaster (*atê*) of Thyestes' adultery, and has continued on through the feast of children, creating the unremitting presence of Furies within. The *telos* itself, the murder, is now also perceptible in horrible glimpses, as Cassandra is possessed by Apollo and foresees it. Cassandra's narrative information, snatches of prophetic future time, is presented in an utterly different way from anything in the earlier scenes, but Aeschylus' pendulum approach is still firmly in operation: seized with her brief involuntary visions, Cassandra presents her information achronically, indeed repetitively, and it is left to the audience to convert it into a narrative sequence.

At 1279-85 material is at last introduced which could give the audience an insight into the action of the next play: a new revenge. The lines are a virtual synopsis of the action of *Libation-Bearers*. However, we still have no sense of where the trilogy as a whole is heading; Athens, the final destination, is not mentioned at all.

The stream of narrative information that comes into the play is incomplete, ambiguous, and disordered in time; by returning to the past, it arouses a high level of emotion about what the play's outcome will be, but refuses even to define its goal until the last possible moment. The narrative pendulum keeps swinging even in the final scene, in which Aegisthus (virtually deleted from the play until this point), fills in more detail from the past in his account of Thyestes' banquet.

Causality, guilt and motive

Establishing a chronology of events is an essential part of the reader's or audience's decoding process, as is the establishment of causality. In both these areas, not unlike a modern detective novelist, Aeschylus' strategy is to make uncertainty proliferate – in this first play of three we should not expect otherwise – as he manipulates our different levels of knowledge. As for causality, both divine and human, very much is suggested, of which only a little is finally confirmed. At the level of theological explanation, Aeschylus indicates many conflicting divine agents at work: the play shows an overall descent into confusion (contrast the clarity of the *deus ex machina* explanations at the end of the single plays of Euripides). The chorus in their early Hymn affirm that Zeus is the supreme causal agent for mortals but at the end, the triumph of evil makes them feel that the god is at best incomprehensible, and at worst devoid of benevolence (1485-7). Only the role of the *daimôn* of the House is at all clear.

This section sets itself to answer the question why Agamemnon is murdered, and teases out three causal strands, the purpose being to highlight Aeschylus' deliberately baffling strategy in this area.

1. Because he sacrificed Iphigeneia

Considered theologically, daughter-sacrifice must inevitably be an offence liable to punishment. The chorus does not shrink from describing the horror of the act. However, in this case the sacrifice was specifically enjoined on him by the goddess Artemis, as the only means to get the fully righteous expedition under way. To add to the difficulty, Agamemnon has not offended Artemis by a previous hybristic remark, as in other versions of the story. There seems no reason for Aeschylus to have omitted an account of his traditional offence other than to weaken the causal link between crime and punishment, and thus make his death, viewed as a divine punishment, less readily explicable.

Aeschylus presents Agamemnon's offence against Artemis as purely *symbolic*, in the portent of the eagles devouring a pregnant hare and, as often remarked, a portent cannot be a *cause*, only a *sign*. He is as yet innocent. Yet a sign might *point to* future causes: if so, what are the referents implied by the pregnant hare? Innocent Trojans and Cassandra? Iphigeneia? Or, from the past, Thyestes' devoured children? The possibilities cannot be restricted or fully clarified.

On the human level, the chorus' lengthy description of Iphigeneia's death omits all reference whatsoever to Clytemnestra, suppressing any idea of the obvious motive she derives from it (perhaps another deliberate obfuscation on Aeschylus' part is that their lyrics generally prefer to focus on her sister). The only possible link Aeschylus allows to be made between Iphigeneia's sacrifice and Clytemnestra's response to it are Calchas' veiled words, 152ff., 'for there awaits a fearful resurgent crafty housekeeper, mindful Anger, avenger of her children'. Yet, like the hares in the portent, it is not possible to isolate a single referent standing behind the personified *Menis* (= Anger: personified in the different context of Troy at 699ff.). They might mean Clytemnestra, or the *daimôn* of the house. Over 1,200 lines pass before the play spells out a causal connection between Iphigeneia's sacrifice and Clytemnestra's murder (1415f., 1430f.).

2. Because he committed sacrilege at Troy

Anxiety that the Greek army, under Agamemnon's command, might behave sacrilegiously in the sack of Troy is raised by Calchas (131f.) and Clytemnestra (341ff.), and the chorus too

(461ff.) keeps the subject in our minds. The Herald unwittingly confirms (525ff.) that the Greeks destroyed sacred buildings. Then, as the fleet returns, Thracian winds (as at Aulis) blow adversely, causing a storm in which Greeks, including Menelaus, either drown or disappear. The storm might seem an immediate and adequate punishment for the Trojan sacrilege – there is no more direct reference to it in the play. However, the subject of sacrilege, now disconnected from Troy, emerges prominently in the carpet scene. We observe Agamemnon's anxiety to avoid trampling his own wealth and his concern to be treated 'like a human not a god'. We are perhaps invited to reflect that as commander-in-chief, Agamemnon, not Menelaus, bears prime responsibility for any act of sacrilege. But the motive of divine anger is left vague and, contrary to tradition elsewhere, no specific gods are spoken of as having been offended by the sack.

3. *Because he comes from an accursed family*

No member of a previous generation is named in the earlier part of the play. Only in the strongly generational terminology of the chorus' 'old story' about hybris in a family one day 'begetting' new hybris (750f.) do we sense a fearful reference to pre-existing motives for murder in the House of Atreus. But then in the Cassandra scene the narrative kaleidoscope is shaken, and new visions of past family members vividly appear with motives for revenge: Thyestes' children (and the Erinyes singing of his adultery). Cassandra sees these visions discretely but, in prophetic context, causally connected to a new one: Clytemnestra murdering Agamemnon. The House is steeped in continuing acts of bloodshed. But the chorus, while accepting that her knowledge of the family's past is accurate, simply cannot connect it to Agamemnon's forthcoming murder and are blind to Clytemnestra's role in it. We learn that Cassandra's inability to enlighten them is exactly the form Apollo's punishment takes. In fact they have just about made the causal connection (1338f.) – but it is too late.

3. The Story: Myth and Narrative Technique

In the final two scenes of the play, guilt, agents and motives are overtly thrashed out. To summarise, Clytemnestra first claims the work is all her own, in revenge for her child. So (1) is relevant. But she rejects the chorus' idea that Helen had any part in it, which perhaps means that she also rejects the idea that sacrilege at Troy (2) is significant. However, when the chorus suggests that the murder was also perpetrated by the *daimôn* or *alastôr* of the House (3), this is a double causality she can accept. Restricting her sights to the triangle of herself, Agamemnon and Iphigeneia, she hopes to draw a line under events and make the *daimôn* depart, an idea which the chorus rejects. They have a bigger perspective and now understand a continuing, generational cause for bloodshed in the house with Orestes as spearhead for the future. This final viewpoint is of course confirmed when finally Aegisthus spells out his own familial motivation.

In conclusion, several stories in *Agamemnon* interlock, with varied perspectives which are not all made available to the audience until after the murder, though all culminate in his death. Causal relationships are extremely complex and 'ends' turn out to be 'beginnings' or, unexpectedly, the outcome of things long past. Everything points two ways, both to the past and to the future. Cassandra's reference to Orestes indicates that even Agamemnon's death – the result of the curse, the fulfilment of Calchas' warning prophecy – will not end the story. At any rate, the whole subject of Troy as a cause of his murder is done with by the end of the play: the central theme of family revenge has been revealed.

Narrative voices

All earlier versions of the Agamemnon story were in epic or lyric form and so were third-person narratives (even if the 'embedded' characters sometimes spoke directly). In a very natural way, the narrator's voice was omniscient and his focalisation external to the story: 'Homer' could relate a council on Olympus with as much authority as a domestic scene inside Troy, or the passage of a spear through a body.

Drama, however, is differently constituted. It deletes the third-person narrator (though sometimes allowing the chorus this role on a limited and temporary basis) and with it the natural sense of objectivity and omniscience that the narration of past events acquires. All the focalisation is internal. In drama there can only be different voices and varying perceptions; situations and events can never attain a final objectivity.

The tragic dramatist has a theoretical choice between furthering his plot through action or through a narrative voice. In fact, although scenes of violent verbal confrontation and extreme physical pain and grief are common enough in the Greek theatrical tradition, battles, murders or suicides are conventionally narrated rather than shown (Ajax's onstage suicide is exceptional). What stage action there is takes the form of ritual activity – the performance of lamentation, supplication, offerings or prayer – or is essentially symbolic rather than effective: in *Agamemnon*, the Herald kisses the earth (508), the chorus make ineffectual physical threats against Aegisthus (1650f.), Cassandra flings away her prophetic insignia (1264f.), Agamemnon famously walks on the carpet (957f.). Because effective action is narrated rather than being visibly acted out, and because there is no objective narrator, the dramatist's choice of narrating voice throughout his play has crucial importance for irony, suspense and discrepant awareness.

In general, voices in Aeschylus tend to communicate in formally structured and self-contained speeches. As Rosenmeyer remarks, 'Aeschylean speech is self-absorbed, isolated, marked off from what precedes and what follows by a gulf of silence'.[9] This is particularly noticeable in the central scene. Agamemnon enters and speaks at 810, only responding to the chorus' address after twenty lines. If Clytemnestra is on stage, he ignores her throughout. When she begins to 'reply' at 855 (an inappropriate word when there has been no interaction), she markedly addresses the chorus, not her husband, for twenty-one lines. Only when she invites him to step down from the chariot do they begin to engage verbally.

3. The Story: Myth and Narrative Technique

Voice of the chorus

The choral voice in any play functions in an interestingly hybrid way: they or the *koryphaios* relate to the stage figures 'realistically' during the episodes, but also form a non-naturalistic continuo in the stasima between them. While they sing, the stage-time of the play becomes indefinite, and this fact, together with their group memory and general moralising, seems at times to put them on a different narrative level from the main action. But the choral voice is never ultimately omniscient, nor can the choral *persona*, in the manner of 'Homer', remain unaffected by the action. In fact the chorus resembles the external audience in being forced to suffer *passively* the actions performed by the stage figures.

These contrastive choral tendencies were grist to Aeschylus' mill. On the one hand he gives them a knowledge and an intellectual capacity which make them heady narrators of the past in the earlier part of the play, while on the other hand he dramatically heightens their conventional inefficacy by characterising them as aged and physically helpless, talking heads without effective bodies. He also gives them the emotional burden of *waiting*, the play's major concern until Agamemnon's actual return at 782. Their voice creates the play's prevailing atmosphere of fearful suspense.

Choral odes get successively shorter as the pace accelerates, until between the exit of Cassandra and the murder of Agamemnon there is no space even for a vestigial ode, only a few chanted lines. However, they begin with the longest ode in surviving tragedy, in which they reveal themselves as the play's major narrators of the past. They stress their authority in that role (104) and demonstrate a capacity to reflect on the complex Olympian powers, particularly Zeus, at work in human affairs. But as humans, their theology is inevitably deficient. They can say only that it was 'some Apollo or Pan or Zeus' who heard the outraged vultures (55-6). They may grant themselves authority, but lack predictive powers, and do not narrate even the past without leaving significant gaps. This past they open up feels dangerous, and their narrative skirts it: they retreat into expressions of fatality, and mingled hope and fear.

The entry anapaests (40-103) and *parodos* (104-263) will be used to exemplify their idiosyncratic narrative voice with its flood of memories, self-suppression, sudden temporal shifts and unmarked movements from specific to general (even leading to what Goldhill calls the 'erasure of meaning'[10]). Their great richness of language, imagery and theological reference will be considered in Chapter 5: my concern here is to show how the choral voice behaves when it narrates the background facts of the play.

They begin by describing the setting-off of the punitive expedition against Troy, a cause ratified by Zeus *Xenios* (God of Host and Guest). After eight lines the narrative is interrupted by a simile of ten lines (49-59, excluded from discussion here), but continues after it to 67: they are still describing the expedition in the most general terms. At this point they suddenly break off, expressing a sense of mingled futility and fatality: 'That's how things stand now. Fate is coming to fulfilment. No sacrifice of any kind will assuage intense anger' (67-71).

We assume the anger is divine, but have as yet no cause to assign it to: we wait to learn. But the narrative has been thrown off course and is not continued. For the next eleven lines (71-82) the chorus only describe their own extreme debility: they are little more than dream figures wandering in the daylight. Now they ask the (offstage) Clytemnestra what news has arrived to produce the sacrifices they see around them. Quite humbly they ask her to be 'healer of this anxiety of mine, which is sometimes malignant, but then from the ...'. The text is then irrecoverable.

Thus end the entry anapaests: the chorus ceased entirely to narrate at 67 and finally resorted to asking for another's narrative – which was denied them.

The *parodos* opens with the topics of the anapaests restated in greatly expanded form. They reassert their lofty authority (104-6); the vultures simile is replaced by another ornithological phenomenon, the portent of the eagles and pregnant hare

(109-20). The ritual cry that ends the strophe, 'Cry sorrow, sorrow, but let what's good prevail' (a refrain to be repeated twice more), mirrors the closing of the anapaests in the way it strains for a balance between positive and negative possibilities. Their voice expresses the fearful yearning of this whole section of the play.

Their alternation of good/hope and bad/fear continues into their description of the portent, which is both 'propitious' and 'faulty' (145). In fact two dangers emerge: sacrilege at Troy (131-3) and adverse winds causing the need for the sacrifice of Iphigeneia (146-52). Calchas' quoted words are moderately clear until we reach the densely allusive language of 152-5 (see p. 55), which may contain a veiled reference to Clytemnestra (though we could understand the lines more generally as referring to the *daimôn* of the House). At any rate, the chorus' reportage begins to reveal, though not with clarity, that present and past are connected together by a motive of revenge.

At this rich moment in the Aulis-narrative, when we desire clarification, the chorus instead break off to sing their so-called Hymn to Zeus (160-83; 'so-called' because Zeus is not strictly addressed; this is a meditation, not a hymn). One effect is quite suddenly to raise the action of the play to the highest religious and philosophical level. To paraphrase, the chorus says: 'Zeus is unknowable, but if I am to lose my anxiety, it is only to him that I can refer. ... He has put us mortals on a path so that we learn through suffering' (this is the first statement of the *pathei mathos* theme, the idea of learning through suffering, which lies at the heart of the entire trilogy). 'But pain that recalls suffering drips before my heart where sleep should be. Though wisdom comes even to the reluctant, the favour of the gods is surely a forceful one.'

Suffering (*pathos, ponos*), resistance, and knowledge (*phronein, mathos, sôphronein*): the chorus' voice longingly searches for a pattern of human wisdom and understanding derived from Zeus. At the same time we are made aware of their human frailty, since their noble thoughts coincide with their bodies' experiences of insomnia and heartache.

How does the chorus' credo, their affirmation of faith in Zeus' plan for mortals, square with the Aulis narrative that then resumes? Critics agree that, at this point in the trilogy, it can do little more than underline the high significance and hugely problematic nature of the choices that humans must confront when faced with conflicting obligations, for Calchas' worst fears are confirmed, the wind is adverse, and Agamemnon is faced with either abandoning the expedition enjoined by Zeus, or of commanding the sacrifice of his own daughter enjoined by Artemis. In two distinct strophes the chorus relate first Agamemnon's thoughts as he weighs each side of the possibilities before making his decision (205-17), and then describe the hardening of mind that follows it (218-27).

The king's unshakeable desire to commit an abomination is heightened by the vivid description (228-47) of his young daughter, with her mouth gagged and her dress slipping off, held over the altar like a sacrificial goat to have her throat cut. Her eyes, though, are eloquent, and the chorus remembers how she used to sing at her father's feasts: once this was a loving relationship. Here the chorus, with steady eyes, does not shrink from giving us the full measure of the girl's human worth, and the brutality and injustice of her innocent death. Their narrative leaves her poised over the altar – a brilliant symbol of all the innocent deaths to come. The pregnant, equivocal phrases with which they 'shut down' the narrative are by now familiar characteristics (248-55):

> As for the rest, I neither saw it nor speak of it. However, Calchas' craft is not without fulfilment. Justice tilts down her balance scales for those who suffer to learn. No mourning before anyone's dead. It will come clear ... As for the rest, may it turn out well.

This *parodos* is for many the greatest lyric in extant tragedy, and it is hard to do justice to the achievement of the choral voice here. By its statement of the *pathei mathos* theme it lays the ground for the whole trilogy. It shows in detail how an ethical dilemma arises in which a choice must be made between alternatives, the omission of either of which will create appalling consequences. The choral voice explores this dilemma at length and in detail, considering it both on the theological plane, as the result of the contingent intersection of two divine demands, and also humanly, from the inside of Agamemnon's head. The choice they describe is an extreme one, nonetheless it bears the hallmark of real complex choices in human life: Agamemnon can freely choose (in the sense that he is not ignorant of fact nor forcibly compelled into one direction rather than another), but he is also bound by necessity, since the choice is not entirely open but only between two dreadful alternatives. The chorus gives the measure of how evil the alternative is that he has chosen as they describe Iphigeneia's death with a compassionate humanity which spells out its horror; having already criticised Agamemnon's changed mental state after making his decision, they now seem to sense that the act deserves punishment. (We might have expected the sacrifice to be carried out with reluctance, but Agamemnon now *desires* it; see Euripides *Iphigeneia in Aulis* for the portrayal of an Agamemnon who reacts to his choice very differently.)

All this the chorus have not only narrated, but narrated in character – old, frail, wise, fearing the worst yet longing for the good. Their story and their emotions, their humanity, work powerfully on the audience, stirring both its intellect and its feelings and engaging them in the ethical conflict. Nussbaum writes, 'the chorus look, notice, respond, remember, *cultivate* responsiveness by working through the memory of events. The presentness of the chorus ... and their patient work, even years later, on the story of that action reminds us that responsive attention to these complexities is a job that practical rationality can, and should, undertake to perform ....'[11]

Voice of Clytemnestra

The chorus narrate the past, supplying voices, emotions and reactions of the characters involved, as well as their own.

However, their male voice has no power to narrate the present or immediate future. This is the function of the female voice of Clytemnestra, to whom, reluctantly, they are both politically subject, and dependent upon for information. It is an unequal contest: while they claim divine powers of persuasion (105ff.), it is Clytemnestra who ultimately convinces. Much of the play consists of the uneasy clash of these unbalanced, differently-authorised, differently-gendered voices.

After her significantly delayed initial entry (cf. Euripides *Medea* for a differently-structured but equally sinister delay), the chorus greets her with heavy flattery (255ff.). In the stichomythia, while their emotional reactions to her news predominate, Clytemnestra is cool and hostile. 'Do I speak clearly?'(269), 'It is of course the case, unless the god be deceiving us' (273), 'You find fault with my intelligence as though I were a young child' (277).

The Beacon Speech (281-316) is delivered as the proof the chorus requires. It and the following speech (320-50) now give a first startling display of her voice's power to engage and persuade, as it presents a succession of vivid pictures to serve as detailed proof. This is a significant prelude to her later speeches of deception. Here, Clytemnestra's 'knowledge' of distant events is logically inexplicable and surely meant to be so, and Fraenkel's rationalising idea that her information is not *ta genomena* ('what actually happened') but *hoia an genoito* ('the sort of thing that happens') misses the point: Aeschylus deliberately undermines a logical foundation, leaving the voice to manifest itself in all its eloquence and power.

At the same time, however, it is a voice that even at this stage begins to give itself away. Like Calchas, she raises the idea that Greek sacrilege at Troy could turn victory into 'defeat' (*helontes authis antheloien an*, 340). At first, this reference might point forward to the shipwreck that overtook Menelaus' contingent, which the Herald will describe. But now her precise syntax becomes obscure and the meaning blurred: '[I fear] lest some desire (*erôs de mê tis*) overtake the army, overcome by gain, to sack what it should not ... but if the army comes home without a crime against the gods, the suffering of the dead might be aroused, if it doesn't encounter unexpected misfortune' (341-7).

The opening elision of the verb of fearing leaves strangely prominent the noun 'desire', *erôs*. Despite a similar prominent *erôs* at 540, we are surely roused to ponder on what suppressed desire of the narrator might be hinted at here? And what does she mean? As Denniston and Page analyse the lines, she seems to be raising three dangers to the Greek army: sacrilege at Troy against the gods; misfortune arising from the spirits of the Trojan dead; and random disaster. It is possible, however, to understand of the last two items that it is the suffering of the dead *Iphigeneia* that might be aroused, and that the 'unexpected misfortune' might be Agamemnon's murder.

She ends with 'Such things you hear from me, a *woman*', to which the chorus can only respond, 'Lady, you speak with good sense like a sensible *man*' (351). There is grim humour here in this momentary truce between the differently-gendered voices.

For now, the chorus believes that Clytemnestra has given 'reliable evidence' (361). But by the end of their song they are in doubt again about the reliability of women (475-87). In the Herald scene, Clytemnestra delivers a single speech (587-614), the first eleven lines of which are devoted to self-justification. In the twelfth line (598), the question of Agamemnon's return – the only topic so far discussed with the chorus – is dismissed. The mood of her voice alters, and her peremptory order (604) makes it is clear that what follows is at least partly for the Herald to report back to Agamemnon.

The voice now adopted is that of a woman excitedly waiting to welcome her victorious husband – but it continues the tone of self-justification. Furthermore, its eloquence quickly ceases to ring true: by any standards, such protestations of utter loyalty, consistency and chastity are excessive and immodest. She herself points up the paradox by describing her words as, 'a boast, bulging with truth, not shameful (*aischros*) for a woman to utter' (613-14), and Rosenmeyer correctly, I think, finds not so much dissimulation as aggression here.

The same tone is continued in her response to Agamemnon's speech; a curious blend of sarcasm, defiance, resentment and self-extenuation. The formal opening address to the chorus (855) creates the sense of a public defence-speech before a jury. She will not feel shame (*ouk aischunoumai*) to use her voice in public to speak of her *philanoras tropous* (a phrase of splendid ambiguity, meaning both 'husband-loving' and 'man-loving' (in the sense of 'adulterous') 'ways'. Her subject from 858-94 is her life in Agamemnon's absence. As Agamemnon himself is to comment, it is remarkably long, a tour de force for an actor, fluent, excited and marked by much grim humour, heavy irony and wild exaggeration. However, at the point of accounting for Orestes' removal to Phocis, we get the sense of careful preparation: two plausible reasons for it are carefully ascribed to the absent Strophius, and she ends, 'now that is a justification which conveys no deceit' (886). But the very denial of deceit raises the thought, *qui s'excuse s'accuse*: the more she exonerates herself, the more suspicion falls on her: her lies draw attention to themselves as lies. As the speech continues, the exaggerations become more incredible: after 895 they are turned on Agamemnon himself: he is perceived in a fast-flowing stream of images as a guard-dog, a ship's forestay, a house-beam, an only son, land to sailors, sun after storm, water to a traveller.

By the end of this speech Aeschylus has fully displayed the unstoppable, deceitful weapon that is Clytemnestra's voice – an extraordinary and original creation on the playwright's part. In the stichomythia of 931-43 she uses it in single combat to defeat her victorious husband. The vocabulary here (*machês*, battle, 940, *to nikasthai*, defeat, 941, *nikên*, victory 942) makes it clear that she is forcing a battle of words. Each line she delivers is a calculated thrust, which eventually he cannot parry.

As he steps over the carpet (958-74), her voice takes on an even more sinister tone. She dares to compare the infinite resources of the sea to the wealth of the House (the chorus have already delivered warnings on the subject of wealth, 381ff., and more relevantly, 750). Then in three extraordinary swift synaesthetic images, Agamemnon is compared to a vine giving shade, to warmth at the hearth in winter, to cool in the house at the time the unripe grape (Iphigeneia?) is harvested. The final three lines are climactic and play on the multiple meanings of the verb *teleô* (= fulfil; bring to an end; pay one's dues; perform a sacrifice), and the adjective *teleios* (= of sacrificial victims, perfect or unblemished; of actions, resolved upon, accomplishing or fulfilled; of a man, one who has full power or authority; of a god, one who brings to fulfilment).

> ...when a *teleios* man walks the house. O Zeus *Teleios, telei* my prayers. May you *telein* what you intend.

Thus in only a slightly covert way, Clytemnestra blasphemously prays for her husband's death to his departing back.

It seems appropriate to end this section on narrative voice by observing that, quite apart from those of the stage figures, the play is full of a vast variety of embedded voices, human, mythical and animal, largely conveyed by the chorus. We hear the voiced thoughts of Agamemnon as he decides to sacrifice his daughter (206-17). Other voices prophesy (Calchas at 126-55 and 201ff., the man who named Helen, 681ff.). The voices of the populace are heard as they deliver a eulogy for their dead (445), or express resentment over the war (449, 456-7, 883). Vultures scream (48, 57-60), a raven sings tunelessly on Agamemnon's body (1472), Cassandra laments like a nightingale (1142). There is even a gnat that whines (892). Different song types are frequently mentioned within choral song – usually to make the point that such a song is inappropriate or undesired: the Trojans' wedding song for Helen turned into a lament (707ff.); the Furies are a chorus drunk on blood singing an ugly song in the rafters of the House (1186ff.); the chorus' fear is similarly presented as an unwanted song 'they didn't hire' (*amisthos aoida*, 979), going on endlessly inside their bodies. These multiple voices vary in significance, some merely adding a temporary aural depth. Others have much more significance: in particular the range of prophetic voices, coming from different points in the past, help drive the action on towards inevitable disaster. As a whole, they greatly contribute to the richness and ambiguity of the play.

4

Gods and Humans

It's the gods I beg for release from these sufferings
Watchman, 1

Gods

The problem of suffering is timeless, and resonates across different religions and different historical epochs. *Agamemnon* starts with the Watchman saying, 'I beg the gods for release from suffering'. His longing for help from the gods is the emotional starting point for a theological questioning which drives right through the trilogy. Less than two hundred lines later, the chorus respond to the Watchman's prayer when they make the tangential but related proposal that suffering has a divine purpose. Zeus has ordained for human suffering to be more than a meaningless passive ordeal: it is rather a process leading to learning (176-9, repeated 249-50). So through suffering, they suggest, will come the Watchman's longed-for release (though the audience have probably already forgotten him) in the form of progress into a better state of affairs.

This is the famous *pathei mathos*, 'creed' of 'learning through suffering', as it is usually translated, though it is worth saying that *pathos* can also mean 'experience' (passivity as opposed to activity; being done to rather than doing) as well as outright physical suffering, while *mathos* means both the act of learning and the understanding or wisdom that results from it. The 'creed' is only ten words long, and the chorus leave as an open question whether the suffering can be merely observed or has to be directly experienced in order for learning to take

69

place. Through observation, *pathei mathos* invites the audience to think that they may learn something valuable from watching the play. Through direct experience, within the play-world of *Agamemnon* itself it is hard to find that the suffering characters have acquired any useful knowledge: the chorus' realisation of the true state of affairs comes too late to prevent the king's murder and the palace coup; Agamemnon dies too quickly; Cassandra had nothing to learn because she knew it all already; *mathos* does not provide her with a means of escaping a horrible death. In fact, the form of her punishment by Apollo thematises the whole problem of *mathos* in the play. If, in her final pitiful lines (1327-30), she expresses awareness of a new understanding of the human condition, it is a very bleak lesson. Nonetheless, the powerful idea of *pathei mathos* remains in the play's ether, waiting to find resolution.

Agamemnon must be taken as a serious religious drama. It is full of gods, whether Olympians such as Artemis, Apollo and Zeus, or *daimones* (lesser divinities). Human characters constantly attempt contact with them: Clytemnestra sets up sacrifices through the city, the Herald and Agamemnon both pray on their return; Agamemnon attempts to propitiate Artemis; Aegisthus claims the gods have acted on his side. As prophet and prophetess, Calchas and Cassandra in their different ways both have special relationships with Apollo. Gods receive a stream of invocations, supplications, propitiations. The chorus, quoting Calchas, explore the meaning of the god-sent omen, they describe the human sacrifice of Iphigeneia to Artemis and, in their odes, lengthily ferret through past and current events in an attempt to understand the divine forces at work in them. Gods, although unseen on the stage until *Eumenides*, densely inhabit the thought-world of the play. They are identified as the underlying cause for everything that happens; they inspire fear, but are also the only hope that things might get better.

Greek religion was not inherently of a kind to support an optimistic world-view. It was a blend of polytheism and monotheism. Many gods existed, but Zeus was preponderant.

4. Gods and Humans

There was a deeply-rooted belief that the gods were the givers of both good and bad. They demanded worship (*timê*) from humans, and when denied due respect (*aidôs, sebas*) bore a grudge (*phthonos*). The individual, or his family, would be punished. The gods, however, did not interfere from the outside with the course of nature (by e.g. visibly overthrowing cities), but worked through the world's natural processes, both inanimate and animate, including human agency and human passions:[1] however intricately brought about, Aeschylus makes it clear that the gods work through Clytemnestra to bring about the punishment of Agamemnon.

Greek religion was not anthropocentric. Man was not created by god(s) nor of central concern to them. Zeus, though 'the father of gods and men' was not a benevolent 'father in heaven'; gods governed the world in their own interests. However, perhaps by analogy with early kings, Zeus had acquired the function of administering justice in the world. This was conceived of as the maintenance of a kind of balance. Action was followed by reciprocal action and 'the doer suffers' (1564), *pathein ton erxanta*; *pathei mathos* is a development of this traditional view. It is important that justice (*dikê*) had, from the time of the earliest natural philosophers, acquired the extended meaning of 'the order/balance of the universe': *dikê* in this sense perhaps underlies the Watchman's opening description of the regulation of the seasons by the rising and setting of the stars.

Something like this was the religious belief of Aeschylus and his audience. Unlike other religious traditions (such as Christianity), no canonical texts existed and there was no body of faith requiring absolute belief. Priests performed sacrifices, prophets prophesied and seers interpreted omens; they did not preach doctrine. No barrier stood in the way of attempting to make sense of the world by rational explanation. 'What happened in the world depended ultimately on the gods, and their purposes were usually inscrutable to human minds; that did not mean that it was irrational, but that the reasons that governed it usually remained mysterious'.[2] If the Eleusinian mysteries and the cult of Orphism offered their initiates a significantly different body of belief which included a mystical afterlife, that did not prevent Greeks from looking at their gods with their eyes wide open.

In *Agamemnon*, Aeschylus is clearly not reflecting contemporary religious practice in any direct way: after all, the play is set in Argos but makes no reference to the important cult of Hera there.[3] His apparently idiosyncratic theology is in essence inherited ready-made from existing poetic tradition, which had regularly depicted the world as a place where humans coexisted with dense numbers of unseen gods and forces. Poetry's function of exploring the relationship between gods and men had been well established by Homer and Hesiod: given that philosophers and theologians in our modern sense had not yet come into being (together with new prose genres of philosophy and theology), poetry is the natural medium for the most serious religious and philosophical reflections of the age. The *Oresteia* converts that poetic project of religious and intellectual exploration into superb drama.

Although *Agamemnon* shows the influence of both Homer's and Hesiod's religious concepts, this discussion focuses on Hesiod. In the ancient genre of 'wisdom literature', Hesiod had written two didactic hexameter poems dating from the second part of the eighth century, *Works and Days* and *Theogony*. *Works and Days* (mostly moralistic farming advice) is addressed to the poet's brother Perses, who is involved in a law-suit, and the poem contains a running opposition between *hybris* and *dikê* ('insulting behaviour' and 'justice'): this opposition, heavily modified, finds its way into *Agamemnon*. *Theogony* ('Birth of the Gods') includes an account of the two generations of gods before Zeus gained ascendancy. It is a terrible story of castration, child-eating and parricide (features shared by the House of Atreus). Hesiod, however, draws a line under the past and firmly tells his audience that now Zeus controls the universe in accordance with *Dikê*, and 'it is not possible to go beyond or to deceive the will of Zeus': the chorus of *Agamemnon* take very much the same line at 160-75. In both Hesiod and

4. Gods and Humans

Aeschylus, Zeus' supreme power in the universe – over humans and other gods – is stressed as a hard-won evolution that will now endure forever.

Daimones

Hesiod's world is full of *daimones*. These are lesser gods, which we would now categorise under separate headings (such as 'concepts', 'personifications', 'drives' or 'forces'), or allocate to different disciplines (physics, biology, ethics, psychology, mere superstition). *Daimones* might be children of Zeus but might also predate him, offspring of earlier, primeval gods such as Earth and Darkness. They have a powerful and often negative effect on human life, 'For earth is full of evils, and sea is full of evils'.[4] Zeus himself has 'thirty thousand spirits, watchers of mortal men, and these keep watch on judgments and deeds of wrong as they roam, clothed in mist, all over the earth'.[5]

Aeschylus' play-world is similarly inhabited. We find for example: justice (*dikê*), ruin (*atê*), excess (*koros*), insult (*hybris*), Furies (*Erinyes*), envy (*pthonos*), anger (*mênis*), sleep (*hypnos*), beauty (*charis*), hope (*elpis*), persuasion (*peithô*), the driver-astray (*alastôr*), as well as simply, 'the/a *daimôn*'.

The concepts here have been inconsistently capitalised, reflecting the fact that in Aeschylus they are not consistently personified entities. The list is not exhaustive: the co-existence of wealth (*ploutos*) and prosperity (*olbos*), given serious separate consideration by the chorus (381ff. and 752ff.) despite their apparent similarity,[6] indicates human incapacity either to systematise *daimones* or to restrict their proliferation.

Giving a one-word English translation for these concepts risks ignoring their fluid nature. Each term merits scholarly analysis, and some few (*hybris*, *atê* and *peithô*, for example) have received it. The results of research yield valuable insights into the ways the Greeks understood themselves in relation to gods and to natural/universal processes.

They reveal very different habits of thought. As a simple example, Sleep was understood as a *daimôn* or external force that assailed an individual from outside, (rather than as the result of an internal system shut-down, as we currently understand it). Homer describes Sleep as the 'twin brother of Death', presumably because both are states of unconsciousness and may look similar to an observer. An Attic red-figure calyx krater by Euphronios (*c.* 515 BC) depicts a scene from the *Iliad* in which the brothers, fully armed but also bearing wings, are about to lift the body of Sarpedon out of battle following Zeus' instructions (at *Iliad* 16.667f.).

Sleep, then, has the capacity to be both external and internal, to be a living force or personification (to the extent that it can be depicted with armour and wings and have kin in the shape of a brother, Death), but it can also be treated as a bodiless abstraction in the modern manner. Other *daimones* have different kinds of fluid qualities: for example, *hybris*, 'insulting behaviour', carries the general sense of a transgression of the boundaries which divide man from god or equally, man from man (i.e. *hybris* can be either a theological or a social offence). *Hybris* in Athens was also a legal offence with a concrete meaning equal to 'assault'. But studies show that the term can be used in a purely interior context without any implication of action at all: *hybris* can be committed merely by an attitude of mind. *Atê* too is similarly both external and internal, the same word embracing both the mind-set that precedes ruin (folly or delusion sent by the gods), as well as ruin itself, the word which most inadequately translates it.

Daimones were 'good to think with' – ethically, psychologically, politically and scientifically. Poetry often rationalised by speaking of them in generating groups: one *daimôn* 'begot' or 'engendered' another in a causal sequence (Gilbert Murray referred to this phenomenon as 'the inherited conglomerate'). For example, describing the power of the wealthy in Athens, the archaic poet and law-giver Solon (archon 594/3) had produced the famous formula, 'Excess engenders *Hybris*, when much Prosperity accompanies men whose minds are not adequate' (fr. 5.9-10). Expressed as a formula, we have the statement: Excess + [Prosperity and inadequate men] = *Hybris*, and every Greek child knew that the next step was *Hybris* + something else = *Atê*: later sophisticates were to see such statements as hardly more than platitudinous old saws. Nonetheless, the formula encapsulates generations of observation of human behaviour, and there is wisdom here.

In *Agamemnon* Aeschylus' elderly chorus are repositories of this already ageing tradition and many of their more arcane utterances become less baffling once we appreciate the typical way their thought is expressed. For example at 381-6 they sing, 'there is no defence of Wealth against Excess for the man who has kicked the altar of Justice into invisibility: patient Persuasion forces him, insufferable child of Doom who-plans-in-advance' (381-6). We might paraphrase, 'If a man does not use his wealth with justice, slowly but surely he will be persuaded into some disaster.'

The extended meditation on the 'offspring Prosperity begets' (751-71, bedevilled by a corrupt text from 766 onwards) also deserves attention: 'there's an old story among mortals that when a man's Prosperity has come to full growth it bears offspring (interest) and doesn't die without issue; it says that insatiable sorrow grows from good fortune in a family. But I am single-mindedly different from other people. For it is the impious *act* which begets after it more impious acts resembling their own kin – the destiny of houses that judge rightly is to have lovely children. But *Hybris* is wont to engender new *Hybris* among evil mortals, at some time or other, whenever the appointed day of interest (birth) comes round, together with an irresistible, unconquerable *daimôn*, unholy Boldness of black Ruin for the house – children like their parents.'

Here the chorus (consistently conflating the language of 'begetting' with the monetary sense of 'getting interest') debates whether prosperity in itself leads to sorrow (by some law of natural reversal), or whether a family's prosperity might not continue forever, provided it behaves with justice (their own preferred view). *Hybris*, however, once it has come into existence, engenders further *Hybris* leading eventually to an inevitable disaster. These reflections are positioned strategically: delivered just before Agamemnon returns, they could not, with all their teasing ambiguity, arouse more speculation about the king's potential standing with the unseen powers.

Like his *daimones*, Aeschylus' Olympian gods are also complex conceptions. The yin and yang of Aphrodite and Artemis in Euripides' *Hippolytus* are very simple by comparison: at *Hipp.* 1328ff. it is even carefully explained that, although gods may get even by punishing the other's favourite, their custom is to avoid direct opposition: all of them ultimately respect Zeus. There is no such neat regulation in *Agamemnon* where, on the one hand, Zeus *Xenios* (God of Host and Guest) despatches the sons of Atreus to punish Paris' theft of Helen in a righteous expedition (60ff.) but on the other, Zeus' daughter Artemis, quite independently angered by the prospect of innocent young lives to be lost, causes opposing winds to blow which will only die down – illogically – on the loss of another young life (the sacrifice to her of Iphigeneia). Why does Aeschylus' Zeus not intervene to curtail his daughter's actions? This topic has already been considered in the light of Aeschylus' strategy of obfuscation, but it is also a theological problem deliberately left in all its baffling inscrutability.

Just a little clarification comes towards the end, when the *alastôr* or *daimôn* in the House is openly debated by the chorus and Clytemnestra. They agree that it has played a part in the murder, but while Clytemnestra now hopes to make it depart (1568ff.), the chorus state that '*Dikê* is sharpening her sword for another deed of blood' (1535-6) and they hope the *daimôn* will bring Orestes back.

Here, however little we feel that Clytemnestra's hopes can be fulfilled, it is nonetheless significant that divergent possibilities are presented. This is not at all in the manner of Hesiod: despite some puzzling lessons in his stories of Pandora and the Five Races of Men, by the end of *Theogony* the world has apparently completed its processes of creation and change: all that seems required of humans, as in *Works and Days*, is obedience to a closed system. By contrast in *Agamemnon*, the world is presented as still unknown, but open to conjecture and the possibility of change. Characters subject the gods to their best intellectual efforts: nothing is fixed or certainly known, but some new *mathos* may emerge. *Pathei mathos* contains the positive idea that by trial and error, by getting to grips with this chaos of conflicting powers, rational understanding can take place – and man can improve his lot.

Zeus and *Dikê*

Elsewhere in surviving tragedy, Aeschylus showed great interest in the nature of Zeus. *Supplices*, first play of his *Danaid* trilogy, contains mighty hymns to Zeus, implying that he would have had an important role at the end. Likewise *Prometheus Bound* shows a Zeus who appears in this play at his worst – a seducer and gaoler – but whom we know finally came to terms with Prometheus (although we do not have the final play of this trilogy).[7] In a fine article, Herington[8] tentatively suggested that in his last phase Aeschylus' concept of Zeus might have changed from an anthropomorphic to a more philosophical and abstract deity. In support he quoted a surviving fragment from *Heliades* ('Daughters of the Sun': it is unfortunate that the play cannot be dated):

> Zeus is Air, Zeus is Earth, Zeus is Heaven, Zeus is All and whatever is beyond the All.

Certainly the Zeus of *Agamemnon* is cast in similarly philosophical terms as *panaitios*, *panergetas*, 'responsible for everything, doing everything' (1486) and the Hymn to Zeus, 'whoever he is, and whatever his name is' (160-1), considers him in the same abstract terms. When, in the following lines, the chorus sweep over his terrible forebears without naming them (167-72), it is as if they are deliberately making the point that the anthropomorphic era of the gods is over. 'Now *Zeus* is the name that counts' (to paraphrase 174-5).

Aeschylus presents Zeus as a semi-abstract cause in the world, who continues his association with *dikê*: when the stage figures make their various claims to *dikê*, they appeal to him. Though Aeschylus does not follow Hesiod by making *Dikê* Zeus' daughter (a role he reserved for Athena in the third play), he connects *dikê* to Zeus' plan for learning through suffering: the Hymn to Zeus itself contains no use of the word or its cognates but, before the end of the ode, the chorus sing *'Dikê* weighs out understanding to those who have gone through suffering' (*pathousin mathein*, 249-50; the translation is Fraenkel's); scales (from Homer's poetry) belong to Zeus as judge and maintainer of balance in the world. At the end of the second stasimon, the chorus conclude 'Justice directs everything to its end', *Dika ... pan d'epi terma nomai* (781).

Does the *Oresteia* actually show Zeus evolving a new dispensation of *dikê* for humans? This used to be the established view (perhaps by unexpressed analogy with the Old Testament God giving way to the New, with his benevolent plan for humans). In recent decades this has become an area of intense debate and triggered valuable new analyses. The theory of an 'evolving Zeus' was first seriously attacked by Lloyd-Jones (1971), who argued that Aeschylus' Zeus was no less anthropomorphic and no more developed or developing than the Zeus of the epic poets. His forceful book, *The Justice of Zeus*, remains influential. Since then, critics have produced a range of nuanced views in support of either side of the argument. Winnington-Ingram, for example, adopts a version of the traditional positive view.[9] He begins by making the sideways move of showing that previous literary tradition provided no clear conception of the Furies; Aeschylus virtually invented them for the purposes of this trilogy. He notes that they, who are chthonic forces (= gods of earth), and Zeus, the supreme Olympian, are almost always referred to in the trilogy in close proximity: that is because they are working together. If at first, the shifting retributive contexts to which they are linked are puzzling, the Furies are finally revealed as the consistent supporters of Zeus in the move from malign vendetta to a final, more benevolent, rule of civic law. He concludes, 'the drama, as the religion, of Aeschylus – and the two are hardly separable the one from the other – is centred on a Zeus who is conceived as the upholder of a just moral order'.[10] This is a well-argued reading of the trilogy with which many are in agreement.

At the opposite extreme from Winnington-Ingram, writers such as Cohen[11] have argued that the trilogy reflects, 'a cosmic and political order neither moral nor just but tyrannic in the sense that its ultimate foundations are force and fear', an emotional conclusion that seems based on an anachronistic view of ancient society. The largely negative results of Goldhill's study of *dikê* have also been deservedly influential. Arguing against a naively positive reading of the trilogy, he impressively demonstrated the way the word *dikê*, a key concept of the *polis*, fuses religious, political and legal aspects of the city's life. By analogy with the word 'right' and its cognates (to be right, righteous, rightful, etc.) and the many ways in which it can be used (the right to work, political right, to right a wrong, the right answer and so forth), he showed how the word always carries an irreducible excess of meaning. His conclusion is that, just as in *Antigone*, all participants in the *Oresteia* trilogy invoke *dikê* with some justification: the word cannot yield a unitary meaning, and the problem of assessing claim and counter-claim remains.[12]

In a recent introduction to the trilogy, Burian sensibly restores the balance.[13] He argues that for Aeschylus the concept of *dikê* has an application wider than the Athenian *polis* and means 'a fundamental, natural principle, enforced by necessity, on the grandest possible scale. The principle is balance, and its enforcement takes the form of retribution to redress imbalance. Retribution comes by what agency and at what time it will, but it comes as an equal and opposite reaction to whatever has overstepped its proper bounds.'[14] He shows how in *Agamemnon* Aeschylus uses the Trojan War as an opening paradigm for a cycle of destruction in which each retributive act of justice creates a further cause for retributive action (the abduction of Helen produces the punitive expedition which produces the sacrilege at Troy which produces the punishment of Agamemnon ...), a pattern which is then fully dramatised through the family members of the House of Atreus in the rest of the trilogy. The natural cycle of *dikê* cannot ever be overturned: but by the end, through the agency of Zeus (and other gods and mortals), it has been transformed into a civic process.

We have only the first play under consideration. The early exposition of Zeus' *pathei mathos* plan makes us concerned with the justice of Zeus, but there is as yet no visible evidence of it, only a series of apparent contradictions. By the end of *Agamemnon*, we have witnessed the separate claims to justice of Clytemnestra and Aegisthus, and the chorus' counter-claim. The chorus conclude that Justice has been polluted (1669) and their final thoughts cast the future only in the form of further retributive acts: 'for it abides on the throne of Zeus that the doer suffer. That is the law' (*themis*, 1563-4).[15] They can see no further than the old law of endless retribution, *pathein ton erxanta* (1658). There is no *mathos* here, only suffering, in the despair and annihilation of the young and innocent caught in this cycle (war victims, Iphigeneia, Cassandra). The play has ended in the triumph of evil and Zeus' reign seems pitiless. Harsh coercion dominates the imagery: entanglement, taming, subjugation, the snare, the yoke, the curb, the bit.

Humans: the problem of 'character'

Until all too recently it was assumed that characters in Greek tragedy could be simply 'read off' as with a modern novel or, even, as in real life. This produced results that now amuse. The great English textual scholars of the last century produced famously naïve reasons why Agamemnon yields to Clytemnestra's request to walk on the carpet: Fraenkel claimed that Agamemnon was a 'great gentleman', while Denniston and Page, in corrective mode, asserted that, 'it is ... certainly not because he cannot say no to a lady: it is simply because he is at the mercy of his own vanity and arrogance ...'.

The naïve idea that Greek tragedy deals with ladies and gentlemen now makes us smile. It should also warn us to be aware of our own pre-suppositions. It might be that we adopt a post-structuralist stance and believe the concept of an autonomous self has collapsed, to reveal only a network of acquired discourses. This stance has certainly informed Gould's reading of Clytemnestra (below). It is more likely, however, that we are still influenced by the long tradition of psychological realism, to which a Freudian vocabulary and series of viewpoints has more recently been added. We might unconsciously expect that a playwright is concerned to convey individual complex character to his audience: *Hamlet, Othello, Lear* are readily interpreted as 'tragedies of character'. But we should not approach 'character' in ancient tragedy with the same expectations. There is, to begin with, no word in Greek that equates to 'character', its nearest equivalent, *êthos*, being an important but much less inclusive concept. When Aristotle discusses *êthos* in tragedy, for example, the concept is restricted to, 'that which reveals a moral choice' (*Poetics* 50b7-8), and is of secondary importance to plot – Aristotle's view is that in tragedy it is action (*praxis*) that counts, not an internal state of mind. And although he regularly discusses the leading figure in a tragedy, he has no word for 'hero' in our sense.

Furthermore, ancient tragedy has a stylised, public artificiality that works against developing the kind of audience empathy we are used to experiencing in, for example, the cinema, with its close-ups and voice-overs. In tragedy, masks, formal costumes and bare orchestra remove 'clues to inner complexity' (Easterling); actors deliver 'set' speeches; the discontinuous mode of presentation (*rhêsis* followed by lyric etc.) interrupts any feelings of identification we have made. We do not see Aeschylean characters in their private world (as arguably, we sometimes do in Homer, and again in Sophocles and Euripides). There are no scenes of affectionate intimacy (as, for example between Hector, Andromache and Astyanax in *Iliad* 6). Characters in Aeschylus do not seem to have any other bodily function except that of speaking.

A further not inconsiderable difficulty is that if a character's actions are controlled not by their internal *psychê* (our

Freudian model) but by external *daimones*, what space or role is left for character?

This has exercised critics. One response was Dawe's extreme statement that the characters of tragedy are, in fact, thoroughly inconsistent. This is so because they are subordinated to the playwright's desire to create 'dramatic effectiveness' in scene after scene: 'Agamemnon surrenders ... only because it was dramatically necessary that he should do so'.[16] Goldhill's more recent sociological critique has negative implications for character too: 'the language of mind and attitude, which one might think to be a prime way of developing a sense of character, is constantly implicated in the wider markings of social discourse'.[17]

Easterling's important 1972 article cut through a swathe of problems to do with character.[18] She restated a sensible approach to the problem of free will apparently posed by the *daimones*, arguing that the *daimôn* of the House does not replace human motivation, rather it shows a duality at work which is not, in fact, at all alien to common experience. Indeed it is paralleled in modern thought where, one the one hand geneticists and psychologists battle for predominance to explain human conduct while on the other, law courts consider us agents capable of free choice between good and evil. But it was in her use of the phrase 'humanly intelligible' that she provided the basis for fresh insights.[19] She argued against Dawe that Aeschylus, 'wishes us to believe in his characters in a deep and serious way. He may not have been interested in character for its own sake, but he was profoundly interested in his characters, whom he saw as *paradeigmata* of the human condition.'[20]

A fresh development in the discussion of Aeschylean character was made in 1978 by Gould. Rejecting the idea of drama as being, in any sense, an enactment of the way people behave, he argued that 'Dramatic personality is like dramatic space, in being 'framed' by a principle of limited existence. ... The language of dramatic persons does not give clues to or 'express' their personality, their inward and spiritual being: it *is* their personality, and their being'.[21]

4. Gods and Humans

Dramatic personality, then, is entirely determined by the physical and, particularly, verbal medium in which the stage figures exist. Characters become intelligible through language. It is unacceptable to consider the personalities of the stage figures in *Agamemnon* as somehow free-standing entities with an existence external to the drama (at its most extreme, the 'how many children had Lady Macbeth' position').

Gould's reading of Clytemnestra deserves paraphrase here. He rejects the idea of Clytemnestra being required to 'make sense'. Rather, '... it is very much a question of aura. It is not that we do not understand Clytemnestra, but that we *feel* her. We have a very strong sense of her as a person, one who emanates from the world of the play and conveys in herself much of its signal atmosphere. And our sense of her is rooted in the play's language and in its forms. ... One strand in Clytemnestra is her inverted, monstrous sensuality ... but [this is] not merely the "character" of Clytemnestra: [it is] linked to the poetry of the play, with every part of the "world" of *Agamemnon*. ... Through a host of intensifications of language, we have a sense of the whole world of *Agamemnon*, not just the "character" of Clytemnestra, as figuring a dislocated and unnatural ordering of human experience. ... The public nature of [her] language and the formal modes of speech which are the medium in which her personality exists ... and the pervasive metaphorical colouring of the whole language of the play ... ensure that we cannot quite detach Clytemnestra from the play's "world".'[22]

This is an impressive insight into 'character' as totally inseparable from the language of the play. The arc of Clytemnestra's development, as she moves from ironic concealment of her real power to its triumphant manifestation, and then to milder ways in an attempt to retain the new status quo, is equally the arc of the plot as it is of her 'character development'. Her intellectual brilliance is entirely the product of her thrilling, dissimulating *language*. Through language too we understand that she is motivated not by internal pain or turmoil (there is nothing of the *mater dolorosa* about her), but by external concerns which

83

are also the themes of the trilogy – by rights or claims to be defended.

Pairs

Rather than developing his characters as unique individuals, moreover, Aeschylus tends to consider them in conceptual pairs. Clytemnestra is Helen's twin sister, and he seems concerned that his audience should consider them together – Helen receives far more prominence in the play than its action would suggest. The chorus' thought turns repeatedly to Helen as cause of suffering in war (225-6, 402, 823, 1453), keeping up her manifest destructive power in parallel with her sister's hidden potential – until Clytemnestra overtly puts a stop to it (1462). Their life-stories are of course similar – each marry a king, each is an adulteress. By giving both of them compound *man*-epithets Aeschylus links them further together as women dangerous to men: Helen is *poly-anôr* (62), 'a woman of many men/husbands', *hel-andros* (689) , 'man-destroyer' and *andr-oleteira* (1465), 'man-destroyer' again. Clytemnestra's heart is famously *andro-boulos*, 'man-minded'(11), an adjective with wonderfully unrestrictable meanings (though all of them sinister) ranging from, 'with a mind like a man', to 'mindful of her husband'.

The figure of Hesiod's Pandora probably stands not far behind Aeschylus' presentation of both sisters as a kind of unitary 'woman-harming-man' concept. Twice Hesiod tells of the creation of the very first woman out of clay by the gods (headed by Zeus), as a punishment directed at man. The name of this woman, Pandora, means, 'the giver of all gifts', and is an ironic allusion to the plagues and miseries she brings, evils concealed by her deceitfully beautiful exterior. Through the deadly beauty of Helen and the deadly deceit of Clytemnestra, *Agamemnon* reflects this view of women as a sex specifically designed to harm men by deceit.

The twin Tyndarid sisters are married to the Atreidae brothers. Grammar is forced to its limits at the outset of the entry anapaests which first describe them, compressing them into one entity: 'a great adversary at law, Lord Menelaus and Agamemnon, the mighty yoke of honour of the sons of Atreus, twin-throned from Zeus and twin-sceptred ...'. Menelaus' separate kingdom in Sparta is elided so that both brothers appear to live together in their family house. In this way Argos becomes the virtual site of Helen's seduction as well as the place from which vengeance for it is exacted; Menelaus' loss at sea is understood by the audience as a precursor of a doom awaiting his brother.

Clytemnestra and Cassandra make another pair, polarised along the axis of language. One of them lies and persuades everyone, the other tells the truth and persuades no one.

Aeschylus also creates some links between Cassandra and Iphigeneia as a pair of doomed virgins. Rehm[23] notes that both cast off garments before death; both deaths are perverted sacrifices, one determined by Artemis and the other by her sibling Apollo. While Iphigeneia is 'a picture straining to speak' (242), Cassandra sees that life is like a picture 'blotted out by a sponge' (1329). Both sacrifices are contrasted with earlier, happier, ritual occasions in their father's presence (cf. 243-7 and 1277-8).

Female versus male: gender and gender-horror

Over the last four decades, anthropology, sociology and feminist studies have all transformed our understanding of the role of women in Greek tragedy.[24] It should first be made clear that, despite the titanic role of Clytemnestra in *Agamemnon* (and Medea, Antigone, Electra, Deianeira, Phaedra all dominate their tragedies too), the lives of real women in fifth-century Athens were extremely restricted. All evidence about them comes from men. Perhaps the best-known comment on contemporary women is the dismissive remark Thucydides attributes to Pericles in his Funeral speech of 430 BC. Addressing the female relatives of the dead, he says, 'Your great glory is not to be inferior to what god has made you, and the greatest glory of a woman is to be least talked about by men, whether in praise or blame.'[25]

The invisibility of women in the public arena is borne out by legal texts that show that women were lifelong legal minors, who exercised no political or financial rights. They did not participate in the exclusively male democracy. They were always under the control of a male *kurios* or guardian – first father, then husband. In marriage there was an imbalance of age: girls tended to be married at the age of puberty, while the husband selected for them was likely to be about thirty.[26]

A feature that brings out their value in the eyes of men is the *epiklêros* system: if her father's household was left without a male heir, the daughter became an *epiklêros*. She 'inherited' her father's property, in the sense that she acquired the right to transfer the ownership of the family property to a male member of the immediate family: in fact this meant that she was legally obliged to marry the next-of-kin on her father's side, even if this meant leaving a marriage she had already made.[27] The reason for this was to produce a male heir for her father's *oikos*. From this we can see that an Athenian woman's status was derived entirely from her kinship with males, and that her sole positive function was to produce a male heir for the *oikos* of her husband, or if *epiklêros*, her father.

She thus, however passively, played a key role in the transmission of property and, in less than a decade after the first performance of *Agamemnon*, was to be vital too for the transmission of citizenship (after 451/0 both parents had to be full Athenians for their child to qualify).[28] On both these counts, female chastity was consequently paramount and, while men spent little time indoors (and were not expected to be chaste), respectable women lived their lives inside, confined to separate women's quarters with their children. Women left home to visit neighbours, to assist in childbirth and – their sole public function – to participate in religious rituals for the benefit of the *polis*. The symbolic dichotomy of male exterior and female interior, built into the structure of the theatre (see Chapter 2), reflects a reality. Contemporary male rationalisations for this treatment of women included the view that women were naturally lacking in self-control and rationality; male intervention, in the form of frequent sexual intercourse and pregnancy, was the best treatment. Such views inform the presentation of the disruptive virgins of tragedy, such as Cassandra, Antigone and Electra, and also the immoderate passions of women separated from their husbands such as Deianeira, Phaedra and Medea.

Anthropologists have made the following kind of analysis: like many cultures, the culture of ancient Athens devalued women in relation to men. While men exercised power at the cultural centre, women were identified with, and reduced to, the margins, linked to the irrational world of beasts, but accorded some divine powers as well. Women's fertility made them a vital part of culture – but they were also what culture was designed to tame or suppress.

Women, then, provided men with a sense of that Other against which the male citizen defined himself. Men adopted for themselves positive qualities, projecting out onto women what they feared and hated. Slater's (1968) psychological reading viewed tragedy as expressing the fearful 'double feelings' of men towards women.[29] Tragedy, putting onto the stage female figures of extraordinary power, exercised the male imagination by dramatising its intractable dilemmas and basic fears: threats to rationality and order, to the integrity of the family, and the survival of the community. We should be clear that, even if tragedy is often 'about' women, it is addressed to men. This would still be true, even if new evidence were to show that fifth-century women were allowed to attend tragic competitions, as they did in later antiquity.

Greek thought, generally tending towards polarisation,[30] certainly polarised gender. Cassandra's prophecy of the revenge murders to come in *Libation-Bearers* is cast in typically gendered terms, 'when woman falls for me, a woman, and man falls in place of ill-wedded man' 1318-19). *Oresteia* can certainly be read as a drama of gender-conflict which is eventually resolved in favour of patriarchy over matriarchy. This is achieved through the figure of Athens' presiding goddess

Athena who, although female in gender, was not born from a female and in this, as in her perpetual virginity and her military aspect, is a kind of honorary male. (The downgrading of the female reproductive role *Eumenides* 666-71 is significant here.) Clytemnestra at the beginning of the trilogy makes an interesting contrastive pair with Athena at the end: negative, then positive, both are women with minds like a man.

The conflict of gender we noted between the chorus and Clytemnestra in Chapter 3 can now be discussed further. Frightening issues of gender pervade *Agamemnon*. The figure of Clytemnestra monstrously combines both male and female attributes within one body, which also includes a terrifying and explicit sexuality. She embodies the perverted world of the play, climactically displayed in her speeches of triumph (1372ff. and 1431ff.), when the chorus note her bloodshot eyes (1428-9). The combination of, on the one hand, her masculine abilities to kill and to control events by argument and persuasion, and, on the other, her feminine skills of flattery and deceit, is profoundly disturbing. Cassandra can only use a stream of beast and monster images to describe her (1228ff.).

Clytemnestra's relationship with Aegisthus inverts their gender roles. She is the man and he the woman: while she guards the threshold, he is an *oikouros*, a stay-at-home (1225). She is a lioness to his mere wolf (1258-9), he is a *woman* (1625) in the chorus' contemptuous address. Goldhill well notes her prominent use of the word *aischos*, 'shame' or 'modesty' and its cognates (614, 856, 1373). The word, commonly used of sexual behaviour, indicates the kind of behavioural control men exercised over women in Greek society: Clytemnestra boldly turns the male concept of female 'shame' inside out when she proclaims that she is *not* ashamed (1373).

Killing belongs to the male domain. 'The Female is slayer of the Male' (1232-3) expresses the play's central horror, a murder which is also an act of gender inversion: in the scene with Cassandra, the notion of a *female* threat to Agamemnon is precisely what the chorus cannot grasp (1251), and after the murder, the fact that a *woman* perpetrated it is an additional horror. The chorus had devoted much of their dealings with Clytemnestra in the earlier scenes to doubting that a *woman* could even have the mental capacity to report information factually and uninfluenced by fantasy (see Chapter 3). Now they see her as a spider who has caught her husband in a web. But Clytemnestra still demands not to be judged as a witless *woman* (1401) and defends herself like a man, until gracefully giving room for Aegisthus. Even then, she boldly asserts, 'This is a *woman's* word, if anyone cares to understand it' (1661).

Aeschylus deliberately kept the theme of perverted bloodshed caused by a *woman* in our minds from the play's outset by the many references to Helen and the War, which was 'because of a woman' (62, 823), or 'through the theft of a woman' (402, prominently placed at the end of a strophe). The first stasimon from 403ff. paints a picture of Helen's arrival at Troy where she brought 'destruction in the place of a dowry' (406: note the inversion, which recalls the irony of Pandora's name). In the first part of the second stasimon, the 'oxymoronic' concept of Helen as a *femme* who is also *fatale* in the vivid sense of a 'woman causing death' is twice extensively developed, first by the etymology of her name (681ff.) and then through the lion-cub analogy. Even after Clytemnestra's declaration of herself as Agamemnon's murderess, the chorus suggest that Helen, the archetypal woman-bringing-death, is the ultimate cause (1455ff.).

In Greek society, women lived largely indoors. The appearance of an unaccompanied female from the *skênê* into the *orchêstra* often receives explicit motivation in the text.[31] The reason given is usually the absence of the male *kurios*. Chapter 2 alluded to the symbolically-gendered configuration of the theatre, whereby, in some plays, the dark, unseen interior could be identified with the female domain, the bright exterior with the male.

This potential is put to brilliant use in *Agamemnon*. Clytemnestra stands at the threshold into the interior, controlling the passage into it. She persuades Agamemnon to go inside in a very particular way: over the red carpet, which seems to represent infinite possibilities of danger. Then Cassandra spells out the particular horrors of this interior. Then Agamemnon meets his death there, inside the woman's domain.

The powerful effect on the imagination produced by Aeschylus' horrific gendered space is vividly conveyed by Hall. Seeing the House as a 'monstrous mother' she writes, 'a psychoanalytical critic might even suggest [that it] becomes itself an enormous, toxic, lethal womb. It disgorges the bloodied corpse of Agamemnon, killed like a defenceless baby in the amniotic fluid of his homecoming bath; he is dragged alongside Cassandra, stillborn or aborted in a sinister parody of a multiple birth, through the vulva-like doors of the palace into the harsh daylight of Argos.'[32]

Many plays present corpses from the inside of the *skênê*. Only in this play does the gendered symbolism of the theatre space create such a powerful effect of 'gender-horror'.

5

Language, Speech and Silence, Style, Imagery

> As for the rest, I'm silent. Big ox on my tongue. But the house itself,
> if it had a tongue, could speak out very plainly. In fact I speak freely
> to those who get it, and for those who don't I'm a blank.
>
> Watchman, 36-9

The poetic texture of *Agamemnon* hits the reader between the eyes, demanding attention in its own right. It is *deinon*: an adjective that combines the notions of terrible, powerful, wonderful and skilful. Inseparable effects of language and imagery combine. Through dense accumulation of adjectives (many of them coined or compounded), mixed metaphors, verbal ambiguities and suggestive allusions that cannot be pinned down, Aeschylus forges an idiosyncratic language-world, one which continuously startles and arrests the listening audience, and forces them to grasp at complex and elusive meanings. It is a deliberate strategy, and the Watchman indicates here the discrepant awareness between those who realise they must engage with it in order to 'get it' (*mathein*), and the rest of us. Language, just like the range of theatrical and narrative effects discussed earlier, is another heavy weapon in Aeschylus' arsenal, deployed to shock, promote defamiliarisation, and to convey a world where 'fact and fantasy, act and symbol, person and personification freely associate'.[1]

The *Oresteia* is particularly famous for its unparalleled system of interlocking and recurrent images, mapped out in a key analysis by Lebeck[2] and described as the trilogy's 'single

91

most compelling feature' by Zeitlin.[3] These images expand and develop throughout the trilogy, keeping pace with the stage action. Sometimes they acquire symbolic power. They may even culminate in being visibly embodied onstage. Language, style and imagery thus work inseparably with the stage action to an extent that has probably never been subsequently equalled; because *Agamemnon* lays the ground for the trilogy, it contains more than double the number of images in the other two plays.[4]

The rich and deliberately ambiguous texture, with its multiple and often irresolvable layers of meaning, creates huge problems for textual scholars grappling with a defective text.

The fusion of choral and civic language

Aeschylus puts two different worlds into a linguistic crucible. The first, choral lyric (already discussed in Chapters 1 and 3), is narrative and moralising, emotional and theological. Its texture is allusively suggestive, richly permeated with metaphors, symbols, gods and personifications, historical memories and associations. It is a self-conscious language claiming wisdom through the extrapolation of universal truths from traditional myths and fables. Aeschylus shows the chorus fruitfully engaged in this activity, but also exposes its limitations. He pushes all these properties of lyric further than they had gone before to serve his dramatic purposes.

The second language world reflects the developing Athenian democracy. Citizens in the Assembly, Council and Law Courts listened to their fellows attempting to state facts as effectively as possible in order to persuade their audiences into a particular decision. They observed how linguistic efficacy or inefficacy affected the final vote of debate or trial. They would have been well aware that language could control the perception of reality, and be in itself a powerful determinant of outcome. Goldhill's work[5] amply makes the case that *Agamemnon* mirrors a society intensely aware of, and fascinated by, language, dialectic and rhetoric (even if the famous teachers of these subjects were yet to reach Athens). These citizens are also the audience of the play, which has been constructed as a complex legal action submitted to their judgment. A trial is staged in *Eumenides*. Not surprisingly the text of the *Agamemnon* interplays with legal procedure – not least in the use of contemporary technical legal terms (e.g. 'claimant-at-law', 41; 'alien resident', 57), the semi-legal structure of the epirrhematic *agôn* (contest) between Clytemnestra and the chorus (1399ff.). Noteworthy too is Agamemnon's measured and programmatic political speech, addressing the problems of a disaffected populace (830ff.).

Aeschylus welds together these two different types of discourse, lyric and civic, old and new, connotative and denotative. If Aeschylus, as Aristotle asserts, was the first playwright to use a second actor and give more emphasis to speech as opposed to song, then he originated that familiar dialectic in tragedy between the more precise and contemporary language of the episodes and the 'traditional' language of the odes. But this juxtaposition is not so sharp in *Agamemnon* as it was to become in later tragedy: the language of the episodes too can be dense, ambiguous and allusive.

Inherent powers and dangers of language; silence

Agamemnon reactivates the archaic belief that words in themselves are not merely inert but active and 'efficacious'.[6] Hinted at early on through the Watchman's triple self-suppression (36-9), the looming power of words heightens the potential significance of every utterance in the play and cues the audience to listen with particular attention. Words, like *daimones*, can have autonomous and independent life once released from the speaker's lips. The Watchman, the Herald and particularly the chorus consequently speak with anxious awareness. The chorus so frequently break off their narrative in the *parodos* that it becomes a structural pattern.[7]

Proper names are a special case of language's power. By a kind of etymological punning, names are prophetic, precipitating events inherent in their meaning (this archaic belief was expressed in the Greek phrase *onoma ornis*, replicated in Latin as *nomen omen*, 'names are harbingers'). On hearing the Herald's news (681ff.), the chorus meditate at length on the prophetic meaning of Helen's name, of which the *hel-* prefix carries the sense 'destroy', connecting it to the loss of resources and life at Troy: she was *hele-nas*, ship-destroyer, *hel-andros*, man-destroyer, and *hele-ptolis*, city-destroyer. They wonder who had the wisdom to name her so appropriately (their own wisdom on the subject has, with typical irony, come too late). Similarly, in despair after the death of their king, they pause on the phrase *dia Dios* ('through Zeus') and suggest that the god's name reveals his role as the agent of causality (*dia* is both an oblique case of the noun 'Zeus' and a preposition meaning 'through', 'because of'): 'Alas! Through Zeus, the cause and agent of everything that happens. For what is fulfilled for mortals without Zeus? Which of these events is not wrought by gods?' (1485-8). In both instances, revealing the power inherent in a name has contributed to the play's overall search for understanding.

The chorus show that *dysphêmia*, the expression of anything 'untoward', is dangerous, and that it is safer to restrict oneself to positive utterances or to keep silent (*euphêmia*). The idea of silence as a safeguard, hinted at by the Watchman at 36, is expressed more clearly by the chorus at 548, 'For a long time I've considered silence a remedy against harm'. Aeschylus' chorus show their respect for silence in many ways: in their self-imposed break-offs (e.g. 67-71, 160-83, 248-57), in occasional failure to press Clytemnestra for clarification (e.g. 263), in their strange first passage of stichomythia with the Herald (538-50) where they do not fully clear up the Herald's incomprehension, and in their attempts to hush up Cassandra. At the end of the play, denied their usual role of speaking the concluding lines, they are literally and effectively silenced by the new regime.

The effectiveness of silence is dramatised in a different way in the scene between Clytemnestra and Cassandra (1045-68): Cassandra's striking refusal to engage in words constitutes a brief but telling victory. For the first time we see that it is possible to foil Clytemnestra.

5. Language, Speech and Silence, Style, Imagery

Words as weapons: persuasion and failure

Language is the power-play of *Agamemnon*, displayed as a sharp or blunt weapon at the service of all the speaking characters. Every episode shows language faltering and failing, but the goal of language and the victory for the speaker, is always persuasion. Twice personified (105-6, 385-9), persuasion (*peithô*) is a dangerous power and an important theme of the play. The chorus claim it (105-6) at the beginning of the mighty *parodos*; in the first episode (264ff.) they suspect Clytemnestra of being prematurely convinced of Troy's fall without evidence and her two speeches are the proof they require. In the following first stasimon they sing with ambiguous reference, 'headstrong *Peithô*, insufferable child of *Atê* who plans in advance, forces (a man into evil) and there is no remedy'. Agamemnon's murder takes place because of Clytemnestra's dissimulating persuasion: the stichomythia of 931ff., followed by the walk on the tapestries, is a culminating enactment of evil persuasion, to be contrasted in the next major scene where Cassandra, who does not dissimulate, ineffectually spells out the painful truth: she cries in despair, 'I wasn't persuasive at all, not at all' (1212).

Both the chorus and Cassandra, in their different ways, counterpoint Clytemnestra's verbal victories by their linguistic failure. The chorus, despite so much fearful anticipation, are simply unable to put into words the fate that awaits Agamemnon while Cassandra, who can verbalise it, cannot do so *efficaciously*. The ox stands on their tongues too. While the chorus refuses to accept both its own gift of prophecy and the truths offered by Cassandra, Cassandra is of course expressly denied *peithô* by Apollo.

The third stasimon, sung after watching the events of the carpet scene (975ff.), most vividly conveys the chorus' linguistic plight – in some of Aeschylus' most striking (and difficult) metaphorical language. I quote Denniston and Page's literal translation here:

> Why does this terror persistently hover in front of my divining heart? It plays the prophet, my song, though none has bidden or hired it. Nor yet, to reject it (the terror), like dreams of doubtful

import, does confidence persuasive sit on the throne of my thought.

In this passage their terror is cast as a song 'prophesying' to them; their heart is likewise 'divining'. The content of the prophecy comes to them involuntarily and cannot be logically rejected: they have some idea what the future holds. This important sequence of ideas is soon repeated in different phrases (990-1000; the translation here more loosely derives from Denniston and Page's suggestions):

Spontaneously from within me, my heart is chanting a Furies' paean, one without a lyre, one which in no way has the welcome confidence that hope provides. My gut feelings are telling me no idle tale, my heart (I mean) going round and round in circles that bring fulfilment. I pray that this may fall away from expectation as falsehood into non-fulfilment.

The two passages form a ring (a feature of archaic poetry): in the second, 'spontaneously' echoes 'not bidden and not hired'; 'heart' and 'guts' echoes the earlier 'heart'; a 'prophet's song' becomes a 'Furies' paean'; in both cases confidence fails the chorus but the spontaneous song inside their body cannot be cast out. Thus twice, and at length, the chorus suggest that they have an inner knowledge of the future. Yet nonetheless this is how their ode ends (in another passage of strained and tangled metaphors):

Were my destiny not prevented by gods from getting more than its share, my heart, outstripping my tongue, would be expressing these things. But as it is, it mutters in pain in the dark, not expecting ever to accomplish anything in time, though my mind is on fire.

The chorus' intuition of the future hovers on the threshold of consciousness, but is denied admittance. They are doomed to feel in their heart all the anguish that the future holds, without the capacity to use their tongues to speak of it; this is their destiny.

5. Language, Speech and Silence, Style, Imagery

Cassandra's verbal destiny is no less painful to her. The fact that she is denied *peithô* is hammered home again and again. She makes repeated efforts to say that Agamemnon will be murdered, and the chorus show sympathetic interest in her own history and full acceptance of her details about the House's past – in fact they respond positively in every possible way *except* the important one: they avoid the truth with a string of dismissive responses: she utters *dysphêmia* (1078), they're not looking for prophets (1099), the whole city knows what she's talking about (1106), she is riddling and obscure (1112-13), they would not style themselves good interpreters (1130-1), prophets never say anything good (1132-3), a baby would understand her (1163-4).

Eventually Cassandra explains why she prophesies without being believed. With unintentional irony the chorus earnestly reply, 'Well, *we* believe you' (1212-13). It makes no difference. Cassandra goes on trying, but even when she forces them to hear, 'I'm saying you will see Agamemnon dead' (1246), they can only respond with a further request for *euphêmia* and a wish that it may not be so; their next question, 'what *man* contemplates this deed?' (1251) only shows how far off the mark they still are. The scene is a strange, protracted display of failed communication, but Cassandra's manifest agony each time her visions overtake her, the poignant bird imagery (1050, 1140ff., 1316), the terrible proximity of her death and the bleak understanding of the human condition expressed in her final lines (1327-30) make it one of vivid interest, stirring profound pity.

Style

All poetry, through its use of vocabulary, metre, alliteration and sound patterns, metaphor, paradox and ambiguity, intensifies normal language. Considering these attention-seeking features, the literary theorist R. Jacobson once defined poetry as 'organised violence committed on ordinary speech', a phrase strikingly appropriate for *Agamemnon*.

Although the play includes passages of a delicate and sensuous beauty (e.g. 72-82, 403-26, 737-43), its more typical language is 'shockingly' forceful and jagged. Especially in lyric, strings of lengthy compound adjectives, some of them newly-coined for the context, unnaturally attach to a single noun and impede any easy flow of comprehension; or maybe the opposite effect occurs, making a single epithet stick out of its surrounding context like a boulder in the sea (e.g. the sinister warning of *androboulon*, 11, discussed on p. 84 above). Abstract replaces concrete noun, and vice versa. Metaphorical language is used with an astonishing freedom (in English literature, Gerard Manley Hopkins is the only remote comparison one could make); sometimes multiple metaphors combine to create an effect not so much 'mixed' as 'clogged'.

Traditional features of earlier poetry are often transformed: in the Beacon Speech, the journey of the flame from Troy to Argos might have been a merely stock geographical description, familiar from the archaic period; instead the flames are made to partake in a thrilling relay footrace, recalling the *lampadêphoria* festival in Athens.[8] Likewise, the simple morality of the traditional fable/animal story turns into the multivalent image of the 'lion in the house'.[9] So too the tropes of choral wisdom are repeatedly undercut to expose multiple ambiguity. The key opening simile of the vultures bereft of their young[10] is remarkable, among other things, for its abandonment of the clear 'as ... so' structure familiar from Homer; the *comparans* and the *comparandum* (the two elements which are compared) refuse to remain distinct.

Similarly, Aeschylus uses existing epic vocabulary, but may also transform it in startling ways. Here we consider the complexity of a single sentence, a key passage, difficult and possibly corrupt (140ff.), in which Calchas is interpreting the portent of the pregnant hare devoured by eagles by aligning it with Artemis' affection for all baby animals, and specifically lion-cubs.

Homer had used the word *hersê* to describe new-born animals (e.g. *Odyssey* 9.222); its literal meaning is 'dew', and perhaps dew conveyed the drenched quality of young at the moment of emerging from their mother. But to describe the baby lions, Aeschylus employs a quite different word for dew, *drosos,* coupling it with an invented adjective *aeptos* which might mean 'not-following' and so in this context 'incapable of following the mother'. In this same sentence there are two more unique words, *philomastoi,* 'breast-loving' (simple enough), and *obrikaloi,* a word which has eluded derivation but in context must also mean 'animal young'. Translated as literally as possible, the sentence reads: 'So very well-disposed is the Beautiful One (Artemis) to the *not-following dews* of ravening lions, and delighting in the *breast-loving obrikaloi* of all wild creatures that roam the land, that she demands to bring about what is portended by these events (*toutôn xumbola*)'.

In this sentence the first two phrases carry the same simple general sense, 'Artemis likes the young'. Why repeat it twice in such arresting and demanding language? We need to invoke the principle expounded by Lebeck, that the greatest number of meanings are likely to be compressed into the passages where language and syntax are most difficult. In this instance, perhaps the purpose is to flag up to 'those who get it' (39) that 'the young' has not merely a local but a wider significance, in this trilogy where each innocent new generation is forced back into a parental pattern of revenge and death (the brief mention of lions helps to prepare for the centrally important lion-cub story, 771ff.). Then, after the arresting expansion of these first two phrases, the third is no less arresting by being, in contrast, cryptically brief; Denniston and Page understand that here Artemis is demanding from Zeus the death of Iphigeneia: the killing of the mother hare acts as token or portent of this second sacrifice too.

It is hard to imagine that the average audience member could have grasped the import of this. However, just a little earlier (134-6), carefully-chosen vocabulary created further striking ambiguity which seems to reinforce this interpretation. Calchas had explained, 'for through pity, pure Artemis bears a grudge against her father's winged dogs, *autotokon pro lochou mogeran ptaka thuomenoisin'*. This phrase is usually translated as 'who are sacrificing a hapless hare with its brood before the birth'. Stanford, however, notes another possible translation: 'sacrificing a poor trembling victim, his own child, on behalf of the host'. (*Autotokon* can be taken either as equivalent to *autois tois tokois*, 'children and all' or as 'own child', while *lochos* means both 'armed band' and 'child-birth'). So perhaps for those (few) who 'get it' Calchas has already pointed twice to the sacrifice of Iphigeneia before the chorus describe it at 228ff.

Lesser kinds of linguistic violence employed by Aeschylus include catachresis (misuse or misapplication of the usual meaning of a word): Helen is *polyanôr* (62, literally 'of many men'), an epithet which normally means 'populous' or 'frequented': here he makes it mean 'promiscuous'. Language may also heightened by paradox and oxymoron, for example Clytemnestra is a two-footed lion (1258), there will be a musicless, banquetless sacrifice (150), Helen dared the undareable (408), grace is violent (182).

Compound adjectives

The abundance of these is a particularly prominent feature of *Agamemnon*.[11] As many as 102 are hapax legomena (words created for the specific context and never used again), and there are another forty-four unique to Aeschylus but also present in other plays. Many of these compounds are bold and startling formulations. They occur in iambic trimeter as well as lyric: Aeschylus often violates any pretence of 'normal speech' by building a trimeter line out of four or even merely three massive compound words (107 such verses out of a total of 876). Jacobson's 'organised violence' is apparent here.

Aeschylus' compounds are coined for exact purposes within their context (they do not create an 'ornamental' effect, as in *Persians*). 'Unbulled' (*ataurôtos*, 245) is an extraordinary way of talking about Iphigeneia's virgin state (= 'not yet sent to the bull', 'unmated'). Looking back to her innocent childhood and set within the phrase, 'with pure voice' (*'hagnai d'***ataurôtos** *audai*'), Aeschylus creates an arresting juxtaposition of innocence and brute force. In the context of her sacrifice, the epithet also resonates with the additional sense of, 'not (yet) treated like an animal' (= being sacrificed; at 232 she is held over the altar 'like a goat'). The coinage richly appeals to our human sympathy and adds to the cruel picture of the sacrifice.

Other coinages compress a noun and adjective into a single word, for example the evocative *nuktiplanktos*, 'night-wandering', 'wandering by night' (12 and 330), used both for the anxious Watchman's bed (he cannot find the right place for it?), and for the wandering of the exhausted victors of Troy in search of food. *Hêmerophantos* (82), 'day-visible', 'visible by day' is used to powerful effect in a metaphor for extreme old age: the chorus say they advance on sticks, 'no stronger than a child, a dream that wanders visible by day' (*onar hêmerophanton alainei*). The phrase, hinting at the future inefficacy of the chorus, expresses all the fragility of old age as it nears the vanishing point of extinction. With its identical suffix *oneirophantos*, literally 'dream-visible', 'visible in dreams' occurs in a passage of the first stasimon which forms a bridge between Menelaus' grief at Helen's absence and the grief of the relatives of the war dead (410ff.: sadly, some of the text here is irrecoverable): like the previous passage, this one describes the movement towards final invisibility and ends with a beautiful 'fade': 'a ghost will seem to rule the house ... sad imaginings appear, haunting the dreams (*oneirophantoi*) ... (then) slipping through the fingers the vision goes, not hereafter accompanying the winged paths of sleep' (i.e. not to be contacted even through dreams).

As already shown by the discussion of 141f., Aeschylus' coinages often reveal strategic concerns which underlie the trilogy as a whole. One area was already noted in chapter four: the *di-* compounds, *dithronos* ('twin-throned', 43, 109) and *diskêptros* ('twin-sceptred', 43) helped bind the Atreidae together into a single unit, just as the *andro-* words similarly paired Helen and Clytemnestra and defined them as transgressive. A longer-term, though less perceptible area of concern in *Agamemnon* is the offstage Argive populace who, in the third play, will have transformed into Athenian citizens. A sense of 'the people' needs to be established here without too much anachronistic detail. Aeschylus achieves this by using *dêmos*, that specific contemporary term for 'the Athenian people' not as a noun in its own right, but as the prefix of various new-minted compounds that then become part of the lyric vocabulary. *Dêmothrous*, 'uttered by the people' occurs four times (883, 938, 1409, 1413); *dêmioplêthês* 'of which the people have a large share' at 129, and another *dêmo-* coinage is *dêmorriphês*, 'hurled by the people' (1616). This last word occurs in a startlingly expressive phrase, literally, 'curses of stoning hurled by the people', a vivid compression for a series of events – first curses and threats, then stoning.

One of the densest accumulations of compound adjectives and coinages within a single sentence comes at the end of Calchas' interpretation of the omen (146f.). This is a key passage, which exemplifies Lebeck's principle. The coinages here are marked in italics, and this time all the compound adjectives are translated literally, rather than being turned into phrases, so the Greek-less reader can see exactly how they accumulate to create an overwhelming sense of suggestive but non-specific foreboding:

> I call on Apollo, god of cries, that he do not fashion any *wind-adverse* lengthy *ship-restraining lacks-of-sailing* for the Greeks, (so) speeding on another sacrifice, one which is without-music (or lawless), without-feast, an innate crafter of feuds, one which is not *man/husband fearful*: for there waits a terrifying, guileful, housekeeper *rising-again*, mindful *child-avenging* Anger.

The dense epithets riddlingly keep at bay the identity of 'the house-keeper, Anger' at the same time as they suggest that identification is of key importance.[12]

Aeschylus' heavy compounds readily lent themselves to parody, as in Aristophanes *Frogs*, where they are described as 'mountainous mouthfuls of words' and, in the ludicrous manner of comedy, found heavy when weighed in a comic scale pan. The fictional Aeschylus in the comedy, however, makes a valid defence: 'Great thoughts and great imaginings need words commensurate.'[13]

In later antiquity, the critic Dionysius of Halicarnassus described Aeschylus as *austêros*, 'strong', 'harsh', or 'stern', saying that his style had an *authadês kallos*, a 'self-willed beauty'. Aeschylus' 'weightiness' is certainly not at all similar in feel to the fully 'classical' technical perfection of Sophocles and Euripides. He can be stiff and archaic, his harsh phrasing can lack euphony, his diction (though sometimes oddly colloquial) bombastic, heavy and obscure. On the other hand, all this creates a uniquely exciting and challenging world for the imagination of the audience to inhabit. Furthermore, sentence structure, certainly within the episodes, is clear enough, and Aeschylus understands the virtue of contrast. He is capable of a telling directness of expression where it counts. Cassandra's final lines (1327f.) are a good example:

> Human concerns! When they go well, they are like a shadow, when badly, a damp sponge wipes out the picture! For this more than anything else, I am filled with pity.

Likewise Clytemnestra's devastating clarity at 1401-6:

> You question me as though I were a witless woman. But with fearless heart I say to you, who know it: it's all the same whether you want to praise or blame me. Here is Agamemnon, my husband, and a corpse, the work if this hand of mine, a worker of justice. And that's how it is.

Imagery

Imagery is a general term to cover the figures of simile, metaphor and metonymy[14] and personification. It can create an enormous range of effects, ranging from subtle and almost

103

imperceptible to startling and frightening. It can have a re-creative power, forcing the reader or audience to see things newly, often sensually. On the other hand, much imagery in language has ceased to be felt as such: in the common alliterative phrase, *kludôn kakôn*, 'a sea of troubles' we hardly feel that 'sea' has replaced a more neutral word such as 'mass'. This is an example of a dead metaphor, and Aeschylus avoids these, unless he can startle us by reanimating them.

In *Agamemnon* certainly, imagery is inextricable from language: many of the single words already discussed, whether new-minted or used in a deviant context, formed an image. The Watchman's bed, for example, was described as 'wandering by night', but 'to wander' is the activity of a human not an inanimate object. Persuasion 'still breathes down on me from god', sing the chorus (105-6), momentarily making a *daimôn* of an abstract noun by giving it lungs and a mouth.

Some of Aeschylus' major personified *daimones* have already been considered in Chapter 4. It only needs to be added here that Aeschylus repeatedly creates minor unexpected personifications, building up a world of multifarious dynamic entities. Thus grief bites (791), fire and water conspire (650-1), a storm is an evil shepherd (656-7), disease is a neighbour breaking through the party wall (1002f.), ears of corn feel pangs of childbirth (1391-2), dust is mud's thirsty sister (494-5). In more extended passages of visionary personification, Ares is a money-changer trafficking in the bodies of dead men, short-changing their kin with ashes in an empty urn (437f.). Meanwhile Justice shines in the houses of the poor but abandons those of the rich (772f.).[15]

The major image-systems of the play, can only be briefly outlined here. One is light and darkness,[16] another sacrifice:[17] Vidal-Nacquet considered the inter-connectivity of sacrifice and hunting.[18] Knox magnificently explored the multivalency of the lion-cub story (717ff.), which is perhaps the most overt and extended expression of this pervasive nexus.[19] The simile of the vultures and its complementing omen of the eagles deserves careful attention: the images there, densely interwoven with associative repetition, create the springboard for the whole play.[20] Most images connect together through verbal similarity rather than strict duplication, and we have already described how the initial presentation comes in a highly condensed form and is presented almost like a riddle (*ainigma*): if the audience could only 'get it' early on, they would be able to predict the future course of events. As it is, they must rely on the gradual expansion of the image as it develops in time with the unfolding of the plot.

Leavis rightly warned that 'it will not do to treat metaphors, images, and other local effects as if their relations to the poem were at all like that of plums to a cake'.[21] The *Agamemnon*'s image-systems interlock and overlap like the circles of a Venn diagram, accounting for much of the clogged imagery; their effect is in their totality. Taking into account the fact that the separation of one element from the whole is an artificial, inevitably reductive process, two examples of imagery, one small and one large, are isolated here.

Trampling

In the first stasimon, the chorus, with ostensible reference to Paris (but some ambiguity), disagree with people who deny the gods' interest in men who trample on 'the beauty of things inviolate' (369f.), and they go on to talk of the ruin of the man who has 'kicked the great altar of Justice into invisibility' (383f.). Later, in the fatal walk on the carpet, 'trampling' becomes visible and literal. Whoever 'the trampler' was at 369f., here he is Agamemnon, guilty, as the imagery has suggested, of 'trampling' the inviolate beauty of his daughter and the population and the sacred places of Troy. Tempted by his wife, he now literally tramples on a physical object that should be 'inviolate' too because of its cost. His action is a symbolic enactment of his crimes and the last example of his *hybris*. Aeschylus completes the image of trampling neatly, by giving Agamemnon 'trampling' (*patôn*, 957) as his final word before he goes in to meet Clytemnestra's justice.

The net

Leavis' dictum is very relevant here: since nets were widely used in antiquity for hunting as well as fishing, net imagery inevitably connects with another image system, 'the hunt'. 'The hunt' includes the tracking and pursuing of prey, the eagles' hunt of the hare, Clytemnestra as a hunting dog, as a watchdog of the house, and as a hateful bitch, and the Fury or Furies as pursuers of the wicked. Hunting culminates in a kill, and for this Aeschylus has substituted the pervasive imagery of sacrifice (as well as a literal human sacrifice).The connections made through imagery are not to be severed. However, one aspect of the net image, which is perhaps one of the most prominent in the play, is briefly discussed here.

Aeschylus uses at least a dozen different nouns meaning 'net', as well as much associated vocabulary conveying the ideas of entanglement, taming and subduing. Just one function of the net imagery (as with 'trampling') is to make an indirect causal link between Paris' crime, the fall of Troy and Agamemnon's murder. The image makes a prominent first appearance in condensed form at the opening of the first stasimon, which seems to begin as a plain victory ode (355f.):

O Zeus and you Night, possessor of great ornaments! Since indeed you (Night) have thrown an enveloping net over the towers of Troy so that no one, full-grown or young, can surmount disaster's (*atê*) all-catching net of slavery; and truly I revere great Zeus God-of-Host-and-Guest who has achieved these things, aiming his bow at Paris ....

Here Night and Zeus co-operate: Night throws the net, while Zeus makes the kill. Much later, in her speech of triumph over Agamemnon's body (1372f.), Clytemnestra says:

How else could one build up a net of harm, at a height too great for him to leap out? ... I put around him a boundless net, like that for fishes, the evil wealth of a robe, and I struck him three times in gratitude to Zeus-Who-Keeps-the-Dead-Safe.

The 'net' of Night and the 'net' of Clytemnestra echo one another; both are insurmountable and all-enveloping, blows follow, and Zeus in different aspects attends. The audience can see the net as she speaks – an extraordinary effect. Again a mental image has culminated in physical presence. Net imagery paradoxically conveys the influence of Zeus first with, then against, Agamemnon. The net by which the king killed/conquered has now killed/conquered him.

Viewed like this in isolation, the two net images seem to uncover a contradiction. But intervening associated images have made the movement from one to the other comprehensible, by revealing a whole world of entanglement and subjugation from which no one is exempt. A 'curb or 'horse's bit' (132) silences Iphigeneia; a gag is put round her 'lovely mouth' (235-6); Clytemnestra cruelly speculates that Cassandra, like an untamed horse, 'does not understand how to endure the rein before foaming away her spirit in blood' (1066-7); Agamemnon captured Cassandra (like Troy) 'within a fateful net' (1048), so she must wear the 'yoke of slavery' (1071, 1226); finally this fate spreads to the whole populace, since Aegisthus is ready to 'yoke the disobedient with heavy chains' (1639-40).

After resolving on his daughter's sacrifice, Agamemnon put on 'the yoke-strap of Necessity' (218). Cassandra foresees his ultimate entanglement: 'she (Clytemnestra) stretches out hand after hand, reaching them out' (1110), surely the action of drawing in a huge net; then more clearly (1114f.), 'Ah, what is this appearing? Can it be some net of Hades? No, the net is his wife ....' The grieving chorus see Clytemnestra as the spider in the web where Agamemnon lies (1492, repeated 1516); earlier, Clytemnestra had jauntily asserted that if Agamemnon had been wounded as many times as rumour reported, 'he would have been more full of holes than a net' (868). At the end of the play, Aegisthus describes Agamemnon as lying 'amid the woven robes of the Furies' (1580), and 'in the nets of Justice' (1611). He is himself a ' "righteous stitcher" of the murder' (1604). The next play will show the

current victors entangled and killed in their turn: there is no
escape from the net.

6

The Reception of *Agamemnon*

Malevole: Egistus, didst ever hear of one Egistus?
Mendoza: Gistus?
Malevole: Ay, Egistus, he was a filthy incontinent fleshmonger,
such a one as thou art.
John Marston, The Malcontent (1604), 1.5.2-13

Introduction

In the light of reception studies, *Agamemnon*, traditionally regarded as a 'fixed' text, is only the starting point of myriad fluid re-workings, made in different circumstances in different European countries over two and a half millennia in all imaginable media – painting, etching, opera, ballet, mime, puppetry, film; burlesque and parody as well as (especially over the past few decades) serious drama. Sometimes the trilogy has been reduced to two plays, sometimes an extended sequence has been created using Euripides' *Iphigeneia in Aulis* and Sophocles' *Electra*. The play has inspired re-workings in which Aegisthus, Electra, Iphigeneia or Cassandra are central figures; or Thyestes, who is only glancingly referred to by Aeschylus, may be the centre of interest. Dramatic productions raise many issues of interest: original language versus vernacular, translation versus adaptation; concepts of 'appropriation', 'refigurisation' or even 'foreignisation' may arise. Currently, in a new wave of interest, versions of *Agamemnon* are being performed in every corner of the globe (including post-colonial countries), and the play is in the forefront of theatrical developments.

From among the diverse play versions of *Agamemnon* down the ages there are perhaps two constant threads of interest.[1] The first is that the death of Agamemnon, causing political rupture, repeatedly lends itself to contemporary analogy: versions have mirrored political crisis in revolutionary France, America during the Vietnam War and a communist counter-coup in Russia. Citizen Lemercier produced an *Agamemnon* in the Théâtre de la République in Paris in 1797; in America in 1973, David Rabe's *The Orphan* (one of his *Vietnam Plays* which borrowed from *Iphigeneia in Aulis* as well as the *Oresteia*) portrayed Agamemnon as a caricature of Lyndon Johnson (the current President), while Aegisthus became a Nixon figure who cut off Electra's hands and tongue in prison to silence her opposition; Stein's 'democratic' German production was revived to play in Moscow during anti-communist activity against Yeltsin in 1994.

The second thread is Clytemnestra: how ruthless and independent a murderess is she allowed to be? In line with the receiving culture's perception of women,[2] Aeschylus' heroine has been frequently toned down, so that she only partners Aegisthus in her husband's murder. Sometimes she is given those qualities of maternal and moral anguish so splendidly absent in Aeschylus' creation. In these post-feminist times, Clytemnestra is more likely to be allowed once again to revel in her solo act and be an archetypal Bad Woman.

An outline history of performances of *Agamemnon* and related play-texts is given in the Chronology on pp. 150-2. The information is taken from the database of the Archive of Performance of Greek and Roman Drama (APGRD), compiled by Amanda Wrigley and published in ch. 19 of F. Macintosh (ed.), *Agamemnon Staged: Proceedings of the Agamemnon Conference 2001*. This volume is a superb resource, and an obligatory starting-point for further research into different areas of the play's reception.

Rather than summarising material from *Agamemnon Staged*, this chapter concerns itself with the way reception, like the flow of water along a river, can provoke one and then another effect – and continues to do so long after the original source has been joined by other waters. What can we distinguish of *Agamemnon* once it is diluted in later tragedy, or when it seems to be present only in homoeopathic quantities? Or when the resemblance is fortuitous? Here we must draw on phrases such as 'deep source, resource, influence, confluence, tradition, heritage, origin, antecedent, precursor, background, milieu, subtext, context, intertext, affinity, analogue':[3] there are, after all, a multitude of possible ways one text may relate to another.

This chapter explores Seneca's 'remake' of *Agamemnon* 500 years later in Rome and then, 1,500 years or so after that, some 'Senecan' revenge-dramas, including *Hamlet*, written in England at the end of the sixteenth century and the beginning of the seventeenth. Seneca may or may not have been influenced by Aeschylus' play; Tarrant, who edited Seneca's text in 1976, talks of 'an almost complete absence of similarity in structure and characterisation'.[4] Yet Seneca was undoubtedly aware of it.

By contrast, it is extremely unlikely that any Elizabethan playwright had access to Aeschylus' *Agamemnon* in a recognisable form. Greek authors were read in Latin translation, and six Aeschylean tragedies, rendered into Latin by Jean Sauravius or Saint-Ravy, had been published in Basel in 1555 and were being read in England and the Continent. However, the translations were based on Turnèbe's Greek edition of 1552 (Paris), which derived from the *editio princeps*, the Aldine edition of 1518, and this had used a form of the *Oresteia* deriving from an incomplete manuscript. In this edition, the trilogy consists of only two tragedies, *Agamemnon* and *Eumenides*. Lines 311-1066 and 1160-1673 are missing from *Agamemnon* and the remaining text has been fused with that of *Libation-Bearers*. So a very different *Agamemnon* results – in which Agamemnon himself is entirely absent. 'It means that only Cassandra alights from the 'vehiculum' and that the reader is suddenly thrust from her foreshortened dialogue with the chorus to the appearance of Orestes.'[5] Yet, despite the supremacy of Seneca for the Elizabethans, Ewbank is not alone in arguing that Aeschylus (in this form) had 'surely gone into the matrix of Shakespeare's imagination', and despite being rooted in utterly different societies and performance conditions, some connection between Aeschylus' *Agamemnon* and *Hamlet* is worth arguing for.

Theatrical and cultural change after Aeschylus

From the fourth century BC onwards our evidence for drama becomes patchy. In Athens we know that new tragedies continued to be written for centuries, but also that an official contest for revived tragedy was instituted in 386 BC. No mention of a revival of *Agamemnon* happens to survive, but Aristophanes' *Frogs* suggests reasons why, despite the language possibly seeming old-fashioned, the play could have acquired classic status: its text was, after all, to survive through to the Byzantine era along with only six other plays of Aeschylus. Perhaps scholars and academics, rather than theatre-practitioners, ensured survival.

Meanwhile drama, particularly that of Euripides and Menander, was spreading to theatres all over the Greek world, and attaching itself to other public events and festivals other than those in honour of Dionysus. Tragic performance became a more fluid concept: individual actors acquired prestige and travelled extensively with their own troupes; the elements of song, dance and spectacle in tragedy increased and acquired separate importance: virtuosi singers, performing lyrics from dramatic texts (and even passages originally composed for recitation), were greatly admired for their technique and emotional expression; in other kinds of production choruses detached from the action to become a separate interlude. Over time, 'tragic performance' might take one of a variety of forms, including a single actor reciting, singing (or, in Roman times, miming to a chorus) celebrated sections from a single tragedy – or even several together: as Gentili remarks, Hellenistic culture (as much in the schoolroom and in higher education as in the theatre) tended to be 'anthological'.[6] This is an age of epitomes and florilegia, collections of speeches on a single topic, anthologies of sayings (Greek *gnômai*, Latin *sententiae* or 'dictes', as they were called in Elizabethan English).

Roman society was subject to Greek influence from as early as 250 BC and at once used texts based on Greek theatre material, lightly or heavily adapted for the different cultural context. Latin writers began both to translate (*vertere*) and to imitate or compose (*scribere ex novo*). While no single tragedy from the Hellenistic, Republican or Augustan period survives complete, we can be sure that Roman playwrights continued the well-established tradition of selecting elements from previous tragedies and putting them together with their own innovations to create something new.

Theatrical Rome

When Seneca composed his *Agamemnon* (between 49 and 65 AD), imperial Rome was in many ways a highly theatricalised environment. There were three stone theatres, as well as numerous *ad hoc* wooden ones equipped with a stage curtain. High masks and boots were now worn. There was a continuing taste for spectacle: Cicero tells us that in the revival of Accius' *Clytemnestra*, 600 mules accompanied Agamemnon on stage.[7] Theatricality was not restricted to the stage: drama sat alongside mass entertainments, mock sea-battles, wild animal massacres and gladiatorial combats to the death. Society at large was theatrical in the sense that legal cases were pleaded publicly in the forum by lawyers highly trained in the tropes of rhetoric; higher Roman education largely consisted of declamatory role-playing exercises, which sometimes included the impersonation of mythical figures pleading their cause in high style with great emotion (*suasoria*: an exercise largely identical to writing one's own tragic role).

In this theatrical city, Nero himself, emperor 54-68 AD, was avid to display his own Thespian abilities (to the horror of respectable opinion). It is perhaps not irrelevant that before

Seneca took on the role, his earlier tutor had been a *pantomimus* (ballet-dancer). On first becoming emperor, he recited his own poetry in the theatre; during his reign among much else he enclosed the future site of St Peter's to display himself as a charioteer, and introduced a drama festival at which he both presided in his box and participated on the stage, acting or singing to the lyre. Pre-paid applause helped to ensure that he won all possible prizes. Narcissism and megalomania apart, Nero perhaps grasped that theatre could be manipulated to enhance his prestige.

Seneca

Ovid had already capitalised on his legal training in *suasoria* to create heroines in a dilemma who subtly, wittily and with artful 'naivety' reveal the self through declamation. Seneca too is a master of this art. By training, educated Roman audiences would have appreciated his characters' emotive powers as they delivered intellectually demanding, brilliant and ingenious speeches full of recognisable rhetorical features such as hyperbole, paradox, compression, assonance, balance and antithesis, together with abundant reference to myth. The less well-educated could respond to the emotional theatricality and grotesque murders. It remains unclear whether Seneca wrote for acting on the public stage or for declamation in *auditoria*. The text leaves some entries and exits unclear and there are problems with staging; however, the play is certainly performable.

It is fascinating to read off Seneca's *Agamemnon* against that of Aeschylus. The ordering of the first few scenes seems influenced by the 'original', but the play then takes an unexpected turn by introducing Electra (evidence suggests that she had appeared in both Livius Andronicus' and Accius' versions), and by giving Cassandra a continuing role: now not only Agamemnon, but Clytemnestra herself pales in significance as Seneca attempts to balance out the play by making an 'equation of conquerer and conquered' (Tarrant). From the start Seneca weaves in plot-lines, motifs and echoes from other tragedies,

Greek and Roman, as well as *topoi* from Augustan poetry. Many other influences must necessarily be lost to us.

The play is laid out below so that it can be contrasted with Aeschylus' version. It is in five acts, the arrangement recommended by Horace, *Ars Poetica* 189ff., and already visible in Menander.

Seneca's *Agamemnon*
Act One
1-56 **Prologue**

The avenging ghost of Thyestes appears from Hades. He explains that after Atreus forced him at a banquet to eat his own sons, Fortune (= an oracle) told him to beget an avenger through incest with his surviving daughter – and so Aegisthus was born. Agamemnon now returns from Troy, so Aegisthus must act. (This story-line may be influenced by Sophocles' lost Thyestes plays.)

A family ghost announcing revenge replaces the superstitious, ignorant Watchman. (Seneca possibly imitates Polydorus' avenging ghost at the beginning of Euripides *Hecuba*, merging him with the avenging gods that begin *Hippolytus* and *Bacchae*.) Through Thyestes, Seneca at once reveals the action of the play and the identity of one of the murderers – a great contrast to Aeschylus' obfuscating opening strategy.

Thyestes makes no mention of Olympian gods, later called 'fickle' (606, 930). Contrast *theous*, 'gods', the first word of *Agamemnon*, together with its opening description of the ordered regulation of the heavens, and the dense references to Zeus throughout. The torments in Hell of the condemned sinners Ixion, Sisyphus, Titylus and Tantalus, whose company Thyestes has just left, replace Aeschylus' Olympians, in whom so many hopes and fears had resided. In the low horizon of Seneca's world, Thyestes loathes both Hades and earth (3).

Seneca's play-world is virtually godless and deeply pessimistic. It begins and ends in moral chaos. Characters are overwhelmed by frustration, despair and uncertainty and their triumphs are futile and temporary. Not even Clytemnestra cares if she dies (202). Although there is a 'positive' counter-revenge in the play (in the sense that much is made of Cassandra's perceived 'victory' at Agamemnon's death), there is none of the *Oresteia*'s positive movement away from personal revenge to the impartial justice of Olympian Zeus.

57-107 **First Chorus**
Uncharacterised Argive women (note their changed gender and detachment from any of the following scenes) develop two further framing themes. In extreme contrast to the complex, imagistic narrative of Aeschylus' parodos, these are plain and clear: (1) kings and courts are corrupt; (2) Fortune always reverses (101-2):

> Quidquid in altum Fortuna tulit,
> ruitura levat.

(Whatever Fortune has raised on high, she lifts but to bring down.)

Fortune (Greek *tychê*) as a subject for reflection is not Aeschylean.[8] But here *fallax fortuna*, deceitful fortune (57-8) – only in the negative sense of reversal from high state to low – is presented as a universal law. Where the chorus of Aeschylus' play had at length, and from different angles, probingly enquired into the conditions under which a man will fall (e.g. *Ag.* 750ff.), leaving the audience to form its own subjective judgment, Seneca presents a closed system.

108-309 **Act Two**
This divides into two halves: Clytemnestra, with Nurse dissuading her from action (108-225), and Clytemnestra, with Aegisthus egging her on (226-309).

The Nutrix perhaps derives ultimately from the Nurses in Euripides' *Hippolytus* and *Medea*: probably already via Euripides and Menander the Nurse had become the heroine's 'stock' companion and dramatic foil.

At the point in the play where Aeschylus had positioned

Agamemnon's dilemma, Seneca now sets Clytemnestra's. She begins with a soliloquy addressing her *animus* (self) (109-10, 112, 115):

> Quid, segnis anime, tuta consilia expetis?
> quid fluctuaris? Clausa iam melior via est.
> ... periere mores ius decus pietas fides –
> ... per scelera semper sceleribus tutum est iter

> (Why, slothful heart, look for safe counsel? Why waver? The better path is shut to you. ...Good ways, justice, decency, holiness and faith have gone ... the safe way through crime is always by means of crime.)

Totally contrary to the spirit of Aeschylus' dramatic strategy, the Roman rhetorical tradition ensures that each stage figure immediately exposes and explores their *animus*. Clytemnestra's thoughts are at once clear, as are those of Aegisthus, who enters to address his soul in a similar opening soliloquy: *quid terga vertis, anime?* 'Why turn your back, my heart?'(228). Throughout the scene, these emotional stances remain unchanged and in fact much of their emotional expression is identical, differentiated only by Aegisthus' awareness of his doomed incestuous birth (*non est poena sic nato mori*, 233, 'for one so born it is no penalty to die') and Clytemnestra's contrasting royal pride (e.g. 162-3, 290-1). At one point she tells her lover that she still feels *amor iugalis*, 'love for her husband' and suggests they could 'regain their innocence': yet all appeals to justice, decency etc. never seem to operate as more than a decorative frill around the inevitable decision to murder. This evil inevitability contrasts, again, very much with Aeschylus' chorus, which had shown a profound engagement with the problems of right action.

T.S. Eliot asserted that in Seneca, 'the drama is all in the word and the word has no further reality behind it. His characters all seem to speak with the same voice, and at the top of it; they recite in turn.'[9] This is so, yet the characters' combination of emotional chaos and detached intellectual analysis, articulated sometimes with dazzling concision or again with thrilling expansion, the whole conveyed through a 'wonderful forward thrust of the verse'[10] is stirring and involving. And if there is little overall unity, each scene is its own rhetorical *tour de force*.

310-388 Second Chorus
The chorus (barely celebrating Troy's capture and certainly not moving on to deeper, thematic reflection) sing a cult hymn in praise of Apollo, Juno, Athena, Diana and Jupiter.

392a-588 Act Three
Clytemnestra with the Herald, Eurybates. He delivers a single bravura messenger speech of 158 verses describing the return of the Greek fleet (omitting Menelaus' disappearance).

The positioning and opening section of this scene is very like Aeschylus' play. Seneca's Herald greets his native gods while Clytemnestra feigns delight at his headline news. His narrative is generally cast as a reversal of Fortune from good to bad (and ends by interplaying with many literary antecedents in its description of the fate of Locrian Ajax and Nauplius' revenge). Coffey describes the speech as 'an enormous rhetorical cadenza, intrinsically brilliant, but too long to be accommodated to a dramatical structure':[11] it may have been written with an eye to independent performance.

589-658 Third Chorus
A subsidiary chorus of captive Trojan women, entering with Cassandra, long for the peace of death and give a brief account of Troy's fateful last night.

The entry of captives and Cassandra ahead of Agamemnon may be indebted to the entry of the captive women of Oechalia with Iole among them at Sophocles *Trachiniae* 229ff., also ahead of a returning husband. The Wooden Horse account has echoes of Vergil *Aeneid* 2.239ff.; Vergil was himself probably influenced by Euripides *Trojan Women* 522ff. and other lost sources, including Cyclic Epic.

Eurybates had given no description of the fall of Troy
(contrast the many references by this stage in Aes. *Ag.*, e.g. at
320-50, 355-67, 524-37, 555-66). The lack is now partly
supplied by this entry, which initiates Seneca's different
design for the second half of his play: he plans that the
revenge on Agamemnon will be enacted literally by his wife
and his cousin, and virtually by the conquered Trojans. The
germ of this idea perhaps derives from Aes. *Ag.* 1279-80 when
Cassandra, envisioning Orestes, says, 'Yet I swear by the gods
I shall not have died unavenged, for in turn another will
come....' The same theme is handled more allusively in
Euripides' *Trojan Women*, where the women's failure to exact
revenge in Troy is ironically offset by the audience's fore-
knowledge of the Greeks' shipwreck, which is a divine
punishment on them. Now Seneca makes Agamemnon's
death 'recompense' the Trojans.

The chorus open on the appropriate theme of *libera mors*,
'generous death', a popular *topos* derived from Stoic and Cynic
thought (589-92):

Heu quam dulce malum mortalibus additum
Vitae dirus amor, cum pateat malis
Effugium et miseros libera mors vocet
Portus aeterna placidus quiete.

(Alas for our terrible love for life – what a sweetened evil given
mortals! – when escape from misfortune is available and
generous death, a haven peaceful in its stillness, calls to those in
misery.)

It seems typical that Seneca has replaced with a comparatively
impersonal choral *topos* the concrete, personal agony of
Aeschylus' Cassandra (e.g. at *Ag.* 1136-9, 1146-9, 1258f., 1275f.,
1136-9, 1146-9) as she faces and finally walks in to her death.

659-807 **Act Four**
*Cassandra, first with chorus in prophecy, then from 782 with
Agamemnon.*

Cassandra now comes to the fore as she tears off her *infulae* (fillets, 693): the same action that she makes at Aes. *Ag*. 1264ff., and already imitated by Euripides' Cassandra at *Trojan Women* 451ff.[12] At first calm, she declares that the fall of Troy is such that *Fortuna vires ipsa consumpsit suas*, 'Fortune herself has exhausted all her powers'. The chorus then describe her prophetic transfiguration (710ff.), an account that owes much more to Vergil's Sybil (*Aen*. 6.46ff.) than to Aeschylus. Cassandra foretells Agamemnon's murder, in which Clytemnestra acts as sole murderess (Seneca repeats Aeschylus' lioness/lion imagery 738-9). Finally, in a novel twist, she prays that the veil between earth and Hades might be temporarily removed so that the dead Trojans can witness Agamemnon's murder and exult.

The chorus now makes an extraordinary entry-announcement for Agamemnon (775f.). Where Aeschylus' chorus had chanted Agamemnon in over 27 verses, Seneca's chorus says:

> En deos tandem suos
> victrice lauru cinctus Agamemnon adit,
> et festa coniunx obvios illi tulit
> gressus reditque iuncta concordi gradu.

> (Lo! Clad in the victor's laurel Agamemnon comes at last to his own gods and his joyful wife has met him and returns, linked with him in harmonious step.)

The chariot-entry, and the whole central episode of Aes. *Ag*. (810-974, the confrontation of husband and wife including the 'carpet scene') are thus clumsily referred to and deleted. The stagecraft here seems inept: 'the apparent wish to avoid a spoken confrontation between Agamemnon and Clytemnestra has been most awkwardly combined with the need to account for her movements at this solemn point'.[13]

The thrilling stichomythia that Aeschylus' Agamemnon had shared with Clytemnestra (Aes. *Ag*. 931-43) takes place instead with Cassandra. Many identical words (marked in italics) are batted to and fro between the speakers in Seneca's brilliant verbal display (791-9):

Ag. *Festus* dies est. Cass. *Festus* et Troiae fuit.
Ag. Veneremur *aras*. Cass. Cecidit ante *aras* pater.
Ag. *Iovem* precemur pariter. Cass. Herceum *Iovem*?
Ag. Credis videre te *Ilium*? Cass. Et *Priamum* simul.
Ag. Hic *Troia* non est. Cass. Ubi Helena est *Troiam* puto.
Ag. Ne metue dominam *famula*. Cass. *Libertas* adest.
Ag. *Secura vive*. Cass. Mihi *mori* est *securitas*.
Ag. Nullum est periclum *tibi*met. Cass. At magnum *tibi*.
Ag. Victor *timere* quid potest? Cass. Quod non *timet*.

(Ag. This is a *feast* day. Cass. It was a *feast* day in Troy too.
Ag. Let us worship at the *altars*. Cass. It was before *altars* my
    father fell.
Ag. Let us pray alike to *Jupiter*. Cass. *Jupiter* of the Household?
(Priam fell before this altar)
Ag. You think you see *Troy*? Cass. Yes and Priam too.
Ag. There's no *Troy* here. Cass. Where there's a Helen there's a
    Troy.
(referring to Clytemnestra)
Ag. Don't fear your mistress, though a *slave*. Cass. My *freedom*
    approaches.
Ag. *Live* in *safety*. Cass. *Death* is my *safety*.
Ag. You're not in any *danger*. Cass. You are though – great *danger*.
Ag. What can a victor *fear*? Cass. The fact that he is not *afraid*.)

808-866 **Fourth Chorus**
The main chorus sing of Argive Hercules, his twelve labours
(perhaps Seneca looked at Eur. *Heracles* 348ff.) *and his previous*
capture of Troy in the time of Laomedon.

Aeschylus had used Cassandra's scene of prophecy to cover the
interval between Agamemnon's exit and his murder. Since the
prophecy has already taken place, the choral song placed here
conveys a particularly strong sense of being an interlude.

867-1012 **Act Five**
The third episode divides into three sections: 867-909,
Cassandra's soliloquy, which is a description of the murder;
910-952, the escape of Orestes engineered by Electra, due to the
timely arrival of Strophius, together with his non-speaking son
Pylades, returning victorious from the Olympian games in a

chariot (artful new use of the prop traditionally associated with Agamemnon); 953-end, a confrontation between first Electra and Clytemnestra, then these two plus Cassandra and Aegisthus.

Cassandra describes the murder in the prophetic present tense: significantly her 'headline' is that it is a revenge for Troy (*vicimus victi Phryges! … resurgit Troia.* 'We have conquered, we conquered Trojans! Troy rises again', 869-70). Her account blends Homer's banquet and Aeschylus' robe: while feasting, Clytemnestra makes Agamemnon don clothing that restricts his head and hands (but is not described as a net); the 'half-man' (*semivir*, 890) Aegisthus ineffectually stabs him; Clytemnestra almost entirely decapitates him with an axe. Amid much gore, the two keep striking long after he is dead. Cassandra neatly spells out the separate motives of each (986-7):

Uterque tanto scelere respondet suis –
Est hic Thyeste natus, haec Helenae soror.

(Each of the two makes answer to his kin in this mighty crime: *he* is Thyestes' son, *she* Helen's sister.)

After Cassandra's speech, apart from her own death, all the material of Aeschylus' play has been used up. Instead, in the last 100 lines, Seneca introduces one major character (Electra), one minor (Strophius) and two *kôpha prosôpa* (Orestes and Pylades), and at the end, oddly, the murderers grapple with no fewer than two defiant virgins.

The little 'flight' scene (first word *Fuge*, 'Flee') with its supplication and rescue mimics motifs from many Euripidean tragedies. Seneca's strategy with Orestes deviates from that of Aeschylus, who had made Clytemnestra herself report that she had removed Orestes, 877f. Seneca instead creates a scene of some immediacy with Electra as a new 'heroine' shown in the act of saving her brother. He also vividly points to Orestes' future revenge (merely mentioned by Aeschylus' Cassandra,

1280ff.) by having the boy symbolically crowned with Strophius' olive wreath and hidden behind his palm frond. Nonetheless, Strophius' so-timely arrival is a little gratuitous, as is the appearance of no less than four unanticipated characters at this late stage.

Between 953 and 980, Clytemnestra and Electra argue (rather in the manner of their namesakes at Soph. *Electra* 516ff.), with some trenchant stichomythia. Electra refuses to yield up Orestes, then voluntarily leaves the altar and offers her body to her mother for death.[14] Aegisthus appears and, against Clytemnestra's wish that he should decapitate Electra, counter-proposes her perpetual immurement (cf. the punishment of Sophocles' Antigone, another defiant virgin). Exit Electra under guard. Finally, Cassandra too spontaneously leaves her refuge at the altar. She will gladly die at Clytemnestra's hands. The closing lines (1010-12) merit quoting in full: the powerful *antilabê* of the final line is particularly fine (and the 'madness' picked up to be Cassandra's final word indicates the madness of Orestes, who will grow up to kill both Clytemnestra and Aegisthus).

> Cass. Nihil moramur, rapite, quin grates ago:
> iam, iam iuvat vixisse post Troiam, iuvat.
> Cl: Furiosa, morere. Cass. Veniet et vobis furor.

> (Cass. No more delay! Seize me – really I thank you.
> Now I am happy to have outlived Troy – yes, happy!
> Cl. Die, mad creature! Cass. On you too will come a madness.)

Seneca's *Agamemnon* is a palimpsest of classical and Hellenistic elements, in which Aeschylus' masterpiece appears only fitfully. Its declamatory style and lack of unity reflect contemporary Roman aesthetics, just as its view that death is the only true freedom is derived from popular philosophy. The play's hellish world of violence, incest, cruelty and suffering is perhaps not alien to the world of the late Julio-Claudian emperors. Until the nineteenth century this version eclipsed that of Aeschylus.

English Renaissance revenge dramas

Elizabethan London was a city in many ways not unlike Seneca's Rome. Barbarous spectacles included public hanging, drawing and quartering, beheading and burning of religious dissidents. Culturally too it was similar: grammar schooling was modelled on Roman educational practice, and declamation was a large element of the university curriculum and of public life. Oratory was practised in the pulpit; the Queen delivered orations in English and Latin, and made a public pageant of herself and her court much as Nero had done. Theatrical performances were popular both at court and among the populace. From the late fourteenth century, Seneca's plays were regularly performed in Latin at university, schools and Inns of Court. The first vernacular translation of his plays appeared in 1581 (Newton's *Tenne Tragedies*) and was quickly followed by others. Seneca was the model for the English Renaissance theatre between at least 1586 and the 1620s (though this discussion does not include plays written after 1607). Seneca informs Kyd's *A Spanish Tragedy* (1586-7, very much the 'founding father' of this genre), Marlowe's *Jew of Malta* (1594), Shakespeare's *Titus Andronicus* (by 1594) and *Hamlet* (1601-3), Marston's *The Malcontent* (1604), Tourneur and Middleton's *The Revenger's Tragedy* (1607), Tourneur's *The Atheist's Tragedy* (1611), Webster's *White Devil* (1612) and *Duchess of Malfi* (1614), Middleton and Rowley's *The Changeling* (1621/2) and Middleton's *Women Beware Women* (?1623).

These plays are 'neo-Latin' in more ways than in being frequently larded with tags from Ovid, Horace and Lucan as well as Seneca: (for example the line *per scelera semper sceleribus tutum est iter* at *Ag*. 115 appears both in *The Spanish Tragedy* (misquoted, 3.12) and in *The Malcontent* (correctly, 5.3). Their subject is revenge (what Bacon called 'wild justice' in his essay *Of Revenge*), often multiple and interlocking revenge (as attempted in Seneca's *Agamemnon*, where the secondary revenge of the Trojans is stressed). In these plays revenge is frequently personified and becomes a stage figure: Revenge sits on the stage with the ghost of Andrea watching the action of *A Spanish Tragedy*; the hero of *The Revenger's Tragedy* is called Vindice; in *Titus Andronicus* 5.2, Tamora visits Titus with her two sons; she is disguised as Revenge, they as Rape and Murder. In the same general way, the hero of *The Malcontent* is a deposed Duke who disguises himself as 'Malevole' to achieve revenge. Very often, Revenge appears as a ghost from Hell: Hamlet's father's ghost comes from the underworld enjoining him to 'Revenge his foul and most unnatural murder' (1.5.25) very much like Seneca's Thyestes: his *respice ad patrem* (*Ag.* 52), 'Think of your father!' seems echoed by the ghost's 'Remember me!' (*Hamlet* 1.5.91).

Elizabethan revenge involves complicated trickery, elaborate poisoning, rape, mutilation, cannibalism and bizarre jests with corpses and body parts as well as plain murder: Seneca's Cassandra had described the repeated hacking of Agamemnon's body after he had been duped into putting on the restraining robe (897-905). Now in *Titus Andronicus*, Lavinia is raped and her hands and tongue cut out; later on Aaron the Moor promises Titus that if he cuts off one of his hands, the lives of his two sons will be spared: Titus cuts it off, but Aaron wittily returns it to him together with his sons' heads. Barabas and Ithamore in *The Jew of Malta* strangle Friar Barnabas and prop him up against the wall so that Friar Jacomo, innocently entering, is made to believe he has killed him; in *The Revenger's Tragedy* 3.5, Vindice appears 'with the skull of his love drest up in Tires'. He smears poison on its lips, and in the darkness persuades the Duke to kiss them. Even *Hamlet* has its skull and poison.

In this world of Senecan *furor*, violence may be turned on itself, as when Hieronymo triumphantly bites out his own tongue (*Spanish Tragedy* 4.4.191). Defiant passion prevails over stoic acceptance and characters adopt madness or melancholy as a ruse (e.g. Hieronymo, Vindice, Titus, Hamlet) or they become genuinely mad through suffering (e.g. Hieronymo's wife Isabella, Ophelia). When the boundary between real and assumed madness disappears, Senecan declamation finds a splendid new home in the transforming power of intense, unbridled emotion.

Banquets and plays-within-plays

The 'perverted banquet' motif had appeared three times in Seneca's *Agamemnon*: Tantalus had cooked his son Pelops for a banquet with the gods (19-21), Atreus had feasted Thyestes on his murdered children (treated more fully Sen. *Thyestes* 641-788, 920-1068) and, narrated during the play itself, is the banquet at which Agamemnon dies. Grotesque and multiple revenge murder at a banquet is an almost standard culmination of these Elizabethan plays: at the end of *Titus Andronicus*, Titus gets his revenge on Tamora by making her eat two pies containing the heads of her sons; Barabas, in *The Jew of Malta*, invites Calymath and his Bassoes to a banquet, having contrived a 'dainty gallery' that will collapse and plunge them into a deep pit; however, he falls into it himself, into a boiling cauldron. *Hamlet* ends with a banquet at which there is a poisoned rapier and a poisoned cup.

In *A Spanish Tragedy*, final revenge is achieved by a play rather than a banquet. Hieronymo puts on a play, *Solimon and Perseda*, whose plot imitates the 'real' background of the play. Disguised as an actor, he is able 'genuinely' to stab the King's son. Plays and masques set within plays are not a Senecan strategy but may nonetheless derive from the Senecan banquet: both are court entertainments. With their theatrically potent effects of double narrative, double role-play, concealed violence and final unmasking they are deeply engrossing: the tragicomic *Malcontent* ends with a masque of four dancing Dukes (including Malevole), with 'pistolets and short swords under their robes': when the music stops, they have surrounded the wicked Mendoza, unmasked themselves, and turned their pistols on him. The joint authors of *The Revenger's Tragedy* employ an extremely complex variant of the same motif at 5.3.

Hamlet

In *Hamlet* the play-within-a-play idea gets a very different treatment: the 'performance' is intended as a test, not as a means to achieve revenge; the 'actors' in the embedded play are not disguised stage figures; rather, the visiting players are new and distinct personages, introduced as old acquaintances of Hamlet's (2.2.385f.). There are two phases to Shakespeare's use of the 'embedded play' motif. First, he heightens the crisis of Hamlet's delay by making Hamlet ask the First Player to recite a speech (2.2.410-78) from a play which, as we learn, mirrors his own situation. Pyrrhus' murder of Priam is another story of a son avenging a father's death, and within the speech, Hamlet's hesitation is mirrored by Pyrrhus': the Player declaims, '... as a painted tyrant Pyrrhus stood,/ And like a neutral to his will and matter/ Did nothing' (437-9; the unfinished line 439 lengthens the pause here). Then, 'a roused vengeance sets him new a-work' (446).

Shakespeare uses this scene to elicit Hamlet's complex self-criticisms and doubts (soliloquy 2.2.501f., 'O what a rogue and peasant slave am I! Is it not monstrous that this player here/ But in a fiction, in a dream of passion/ Could force his soul so to his own conceit ...'). It is only now that he decides on a 'trial by play' since, after all, 'The spirit that I have seen (his father's ghost)/ May be a devil – and the devil hath power/ T'assume a pleasing shape. Yea, and perhaps,/ ... Abuses me to damn me' (2.2.551ff.).

The Mousetrap, which Hamlet asks the players to perform, is, he says, 'a very choice Italian play', 'the image of a murder done in Vienna' – but also (he is using Hieronymo's tactic) the image of his father's murder. Hamlet wants his own lines inserted into the text, and it is an open question whether Shakespeare temporarily provoked his audience to imagine that Hamlet might, if he felt the case against Claudius sufficiently proved at that point, rise up to challenge and kill him. Of course we never know, because the performance is cut short. But we know from the dumb show that the action begins with a loving queen laying her husband to sleep; he is poisoned and the queen is then successfully wooed by his murderer: surely in the fashion of the plays of the day, the audience would then expect a counter-murder?

While it is playing, Hamlet, Ophelia, Gertrude and Claudius make running comments. This forces the embedded stage action into ' "real" clock-time', and there is an excitingly heightened reality effect – created by this redoubled fiction of a play-within-a-play. When Claudius interrupts it, there is a real sense of shock as single 'play-time' re-establishes itself.

Hamlet now *believes* he has proof of his uncle's guilt: 'O good Horatio, I'll take the ghost's word for a thousand pound' (3.2.260). But since he misses Claudius' confession before the altar (3.3.36f.), he is excluded from the audience's *knowledge* of it. All this feeds into the dilemma of revenge presented in the play through Hamlet's indecision.

Hamlet and Aeschylus' *Agamemnon*

Hamlet is much the most complex and fascinating of all these Senecan dramas, with their Hadean revenge plots, exhilarating rhetoric and grotesque spectacle. As superb theatrical devices, the broken-off performance of *The Mousetrap* can be compared with the carpet scene: both are richly theatrical and powerfully ambiguous 'staged' tests of guilt, deceitfully enacted by one character seeking revenge upon another, with the audience's fearful awareness that they cannot fully understand what is happening, nor predict what will happen next.

As is often noted, *Hamlet*'s family story closely mirrors both *Agamemnons:* a warrior king (Agamemnon/ Hamlet's father) is killed by a scheming cousin (Aegisthus/ Claudius) and an adulterous queen (Clytemnestra/ Gertrude), leaving the son (Orestes/ Hamlet) to exact revenge. With Seneca there are some interesting textual parallels too: in particular the mother-daughter quarrel between Clytemnestra and Electra (Sen. *Ag.* 953-65) has been called a 'striking anticipation' of *Hamlet* 3.4.8-18, a mother-son quarrel between Gertrude and Hamlet. Both children challenge their mother with adultery, express loyalty to their murdered father and contrast him with a degenerate husband. Both passages are characterised by competitive echoing.[15]

But despite points of similarity with Seneca, *Hamlet* nonetheless transforms revenge drama. This transformation is largely achieved through the particular nature of its central figure. Miola sees Hamlet as a figure conflicted between Stoic reason and the revenger's passion. (A phenomenon possibly arising from the rhetorical practice, common to Romans and Elizabethans, of arguing *in utramque partem*, 'both sides of a case'.) Hamlet propounds paradoxes, quips and retorts in a way that resembles the dictes of the philosophers; the Greek maxim, 'know thyself', adopted by Stoics (Sen. *Consolatio ad Marciam* 11.3) gives him the mandate for self-examination and meditation which is the correct Stoic response to *contumelia*, 'the proud man's contumely' (3.1.71f.), the outrages of Fortune. He praises Horatio for not being 'passion's slave' (3.2.61-4). Yet passion is exactly the theme he explores with the players, and he is all passion at the loss of Ophelia. In short, he vacillates between two Senecan ideals: the *apatheia* or detachment of philosophy, and the passionate action of tragedy: between the two, a new kind of hero is generated.[16]

Although this insight into Hamlet is based on two different aspects of Seneca, it nonetheless provides the means of bypassing Seneca and other Elizabethan revenge-dramas and of tracing some direct confluence between Aeschylus' *Agamemnon* and Shakespeare's *Hamlet*. Given that Seneca dramatised the same myth as Aeschylus, and that it was Seneca that Shakespeare knew, arguments for direct links based on resemblance of family or plot seem futile (even though mythical, psychological and structural arguments have all been adduced in the attempt).[17] Even if *Agamemnon* and *Hamlet* can both be called revenge dramas, they do not, after all, much resemble one another.

However, there is one shared feature that it is well worth arguing for: the nature of the central figures, the chorus and Hamlet. Both, despite suffering acutely from apprehension and uncertainty, are continually engaged in the struggle to make sense of the world around them, to act rightly and to link human life to their god or gods. Both, against all the odds, make a serious appeal to the possibility of an ordered and uncorrupted society. Although Hamlet can actively seek order through the creation of fictions like the *Mousetrap*, while the chorus of old men can only try to understand by using traditional wisdom and their own reflections, yet the deep and anguished reflection of each casts a brilliant moral and intellectual light onto the deeds of revenge. It is here that *Agamemnon* and *Hamlet* connect – in the stirring dramatisation of their passionate mental effort.

Notes

1. Orientation: Aeschylus, Athens and Dramatic Poetry

1. Cf. *Odyssey* 4.351ff.

2. Herington, *Poetry into Drama* is the fullest treatment; Easterling, 'A Show for Dionysus' discusses the extent to which tragedy was 'Dionysiac'.

3. Aristotle *Poetics* 4.1449a.

4. Garvie, 'Aeschylus' Simple Plots', p. 105.

5. See Carey, *Democracy* 18ff. for a brief and lucid account of this. Primary sources and secondary literature are to be found in Robinson (ed.), *Ancient Greek Democracy*, pp. 76-151.

6. A theory discussed by Cartledge, ' "Deep Plays" ', p. 22ff.

7. This was a form of glamorous public taxation, whereby wealthy citizens financed something to the city's benefit. Some of these *leitourgiai* were military, others civic. Payment for the chorus, the most expensive part of a drama production, was called *chorêgia*. On *chorêgia*, see P. Wilson, *The Athenian Institution of the Khorêgia: the chorus, the city and the stage* (Cambridge, 2000).

8. See Goldhill, 'The Language of Tragedy', p. 59ff. on this point. On the arrangements for the City or Great Dionysia drama festival in general, see Pickard-Cambridge, *Dramatic Festivals* (primary sources and discussion, ch. 2, p. 57ff.) and Goldhill, 'The Great Dionysia'.

9. This did not always continue to be the case in tragedy. Hall's *Inventing the Barbarian* (Oxford, 1989) describes the gradual appearance of xenophobia and more blatant patriotism in the later years of the fifth century. Mills' book, *Theseus, Tragedy and the Athenian Empire* (Oxford, 1997), explores the figure of Theseus in three tragedies and concludes that the hero reflects 'an unambiguously favourable self-image' which reaffirms for the audience 'their heroic ancestry and the Athenian way of life' (p. 264).

10. Nussbaum, *Fragility*, Preface, p. xxvii.

11. For contrasting views on this see Henderson, 'Women and the Athenian Dramatic Festivals', *Transactions of the American Philological Association* 121 (1991), pp. 133-47 and Goldhill, 'Language of Tragedy'.

12. Denniston and Page, Introduction, p. xxxix.

13. For a discussion of the evidence for reconstructing the Danaid trilogy, of which *Suppliants* was the first play, see A.F. Garvie, *Aeschylus' Supplices: Play and Trilogy* (Cambridge, 1969), p. 163ff.

14. See M. Griffith, *The Authenticity of Prometheus Bound* (Cambridge, 1977). Evidence for the trilogy is discussed in M. Griffith, *Aeschylus Prometheus Bound* (Cambridge, 1983), pp. 281-305.

15. A.N. Michelini, *Tradition and Dramatic Form in the Persians of Aeschylus* (Leiden, 1982), well exposes the fatuity of assuming any clear linear development in respect of the formal elements of the new genre of tragedy.

16. Buxton, *Complete World*, p. 18.

17. This long-standing view receives recent endorsement from B. Graziosi in *Inventing Homer: The Early Reception of the Epic* (Cambridge, 2002), p. 246.

18. Athenaeus (*fl. c.* 200 AD), *Deipnosophistae* (= 'The Learned Banquet') VIII 347e.

19. See Fraenkel's valuable and sensitive analysis of this scene: Fraenkel, *Aeschylus Agamemnon*, pp. 487-8.

20. Pickard-Cambridge, *Dramatic Festivals*, p. 139.

21. Given that *Agamemnon* contains some of the greatest surviving poetry in ancient Greek, it is most regrettable that there is no space for a proper discussion of metre in this book. However, there are several good introductory handbooks on the subject, such as M.L. West's *Introduction to Greek Metre* (Oxford, 1986), as well as the excellent metrical appendix in *The Cambridge History of Classical Literature* (*CHCL*), vol. 1. Though metre appears a dry technical subject, the ability to 'hear' the rhythmical patterns against the sound of the words makes the effort highly rewarding. Ancient poetry, which was written to move the ear not the eye, cannot be fully appreciated without it.

There is a tape of extracts from *Agamemnon,* performed by Bradfield College. It is available for hire from Resources for Classics, 0845 456 0992, http://resources-for-classics.co.uk, info@resources-for-classics.co.uk.

2. Theatrical Space

1. Taplin, *Stagecraft* and *Greek Tragedy in Action*.

2. Rosenmeyer, *The Art of Aeschylus,* pp. 116-17.

3. 'Lure-murder' is a term used to describe these deaths-by-deceit in Goward, *Telling Tragedy,* pp. 32-6.

4. Knox, 'Aeschylus and the Third Actor', p. 42.

5. A glance at the lexicon entry makes clear the many senses of *oikos*; there is also a good entry under *household* in *The Oxford Classical Dictionary* (3rd edn 1996, ed. Hornblower and Spawforth).

See also the brief account in P.V. Jones (ed.), *World of Athens* (Cambridge, 1984), p. 157ff.

3. The Story: Myth and Narrative Technique

1. See L.M. Slatkin, 'Metis and Composition by Theme', pp. 227f. in S.L. Schein (ed.), *Reading the Odyssey* (Princeton, 1996) and C. Segal, 'Kleos and its Ironies', p. 208f. in the same volume.

2. The surviving fragments of the Epic Cycle, translated with discussion, may be found in Davies, *The Epic Cycle*.

3. *Pythian XI* was probably first performed sixteen years before *Agamemnon* in 474, although the scholiast does also offer a later date of 454.

4. March, 'The Creative Poet', pp. 79-118.

5. Prince, *Dictionary of Narratology*, pp. 94-5.

6. Rabinowitz, 'What's Hecuba?' and 'Truth in Fiction'.

7. Goldhill, *Reading Greek Tragedy*, p. 6 terms the effect 'the progressive undercutting of the secure exchange of language'.

8. Goward, *Telling Tragedy*, p. 60f.

9. Rosenmeyer, *Art*, p. 189.

10. Goldhill, *Language*, p. 15.

11. Nussbaum, *Fragility*, p. 47.

4. Gods and Humans

1. See Lloyd-Jones, *Justice*.

2. ibid., 162.

3. Contrast the 'realistic' treatment of Euripides in the *parodos* of *Electra,* where the chorus of Argive girls offer to lend Electra a dress to wear at Hera's festival.

4. Hesiod, *Works and Days*, 101.

5. ibid., 252-5.

6. The similarity is a modern view: the fact that *olbos* and *ploutos* are contrasted within the same sentence at *Persians* 161-4 seems rather to indicate a tradition of difference. As Harrison notes (correspondence), there is 'a principle of unknowability' at work.

7. For thoughts on the possible course of the Danaid trilogy of which *Supplices* is the first play, see A.F. Garvie, *Aeschylus' Supplices: Play and Trilogy* (Cambridge, 1969), p. 163ff.; for more on the Prometheus plays, see M. Griffith, *The Authenticity of the Prometheus Bound* (Cambridge, 1977), and pp. 281-305 in M. Griffith, *Aeschylus, Prometheus Bound* (Cambridge, 1983).

8. Herington, 'Aeschylus: The Last Phase'.

9. Winnington-Ingram, *Studies*; Podlecki and Stanford also adopt their own versions of the traditional positive view.

10. Winnington-Ingram, *Studies*, p. 155.

11. Cohen, 'Theodicy'.

12. Goldhill, *Reading Greek Tragedy*.

13. Shapiro and Burian, *Aeschylus, The Oresteia*.

14. ibid., pp. 6-7.

15. See Pindar *Nemean IV* 31-2 for a similarly worded sentiment.

16. Dawe, 'Inconsistency', p. 50.

17. Goldhill, *Reading Greek Tragedy*, p. 180.

18. Easterling, 'Presentation of Character'.

19. See now also Easterling 'Constructing Character', pp. 83-99.

20. Easterling, 'Presentation of Character' p. 6.

21. Gould, 'Dramatic Character', p. 44.

22. ibid., pp. 59-60.

23. Rehm, *The Play of Space*.

24. Foley's classic exposition of 1981, 'The Conception of Women', has been followed by many others but is still worth reading.

25. Thucydides II.46.

26. See S. Blundell, *Women in Ancient Greece* (British Museum Press, 1995), ch. 11.

27. ibid., p. 117.

28. See Carey, *Democracy*, p. 37.

29. P.E. Slater, *The Glory of Hera* (Boston, 1968).

30. See Lloyd, *The agon in Euripides*.

31. Though this is not invariably so, but will always depend on the symbolic configuration of the theatre space. For an excellent view on this see Easterling, 'Women in Tragic Space'.

32. Hall, 'Eating Children'.

5. Language, Speech and Silence, Style, Imagery

1. Stanford, *Aeschylus in his Style,* p. 86.

2. Lebeck, *The Oresteia*.

3. Zeitlin, 'The Motif', p. 463.

4. Earp, *Style,* p. 98.

5. Goldhill, *Reading Greek Tragedy*.

6. Roberts, *Apollo*, p. 21.

7. Lebeck, *The Oresteia,* p. 31.

8. See Ferrari, 'Figures in the Text'.

9. This receives a superb analysis from Knox, 'The Lion in the House'; see also Goldhill, *Oresteia*.

10. The simile is well analysed by Lebeck.

11. See Earp, *Style,* whose figures are quoted here.

12. See Goldhill, *Oresteia,* p. 74f., for a fuller analysis of the ambiguity and thematic significance of this passage.

13. Aristophanes, *Frogs* 1059.

14. Metonymy (literally, 'change of name') may be simply defined as a practice of calling something not by its direct name but by something with which it is associated. A poem by James Shirley (Song from *The Contention of Ajax and Ulysses*) includes the lines 'Sceptre and Crown/ Must tumble down/ And in the dust be equal made/ With the poor crooked Scythe and Spade'. Here monarchs are designated by their attributes of sceptre and crown, peasants by the scythe and spade.

15. See Stanford, *Aeschylus in his Style.*

16. Peradotto, Gantz.

17. Zeitlin, 'The Motif of the Corrupted Sacrifice' and 'Postcript'.

18. Vidal-Nacquet, 'Hunting and Sacrifice'.

19. Knox, 'The Lion'.

20. Lebeck, *Oresteia.*

21. F.R. Leavis, 'Imagery and Movement, *Scrutiny,* 1945.

6. The Reception of Agamemnon

1. Michelakis, 'Agamemnon(s) in Performance'.

2. Hall, 'Clytemnestra versus her Senecan Tradition'.

3. Miola, *Shakespeare,* p. 7.

4. Tarrant, *Seneca Agamemnon,* p. 215.

5. Ewbank, 'Striking too Short'.

6. Gentili, *Theatrical Performances,* p. 21.

7. Cicero, *ad Familiares* 7.1.2, but very likely an exaggeration.

8. It seems to begin as a minor *topos* in Euripides' 'recognition-thrillers' (e.g. *Ion* 1512-15, *Helen* 711-12, *Iphigeneia in Tauris* 721-2), where the vital identification of kin is made to hang excitingly on the operation of chance.

9. *Seneca, his Tenne Tragedies,* edited by Thomas Newton, with an Introduction by T.S. Eliot (London, 1927), Introduction, p. ix.

10. Herington, 'Senecan Tragedy'.

11. Coffey, 'Seneca and His Tragedies'.

12. See Easterling, 'Agamemnon for the Ancients'.

13. See Tarrant ad loc., who also suggests that a dumb-show might have taken place while these lines were spoken.

14. This seems a brief echo of Polyxena, Euripides *Hecuba* 557f. – in both texts two alternate entry points for the weapon are suggested.

15. Miola, *Shakespeare,* p. 49.

16. ibid., p.54ff.

17. ibid., p. 49ff.

The Plays of Aeschylus

Extant plays are shown in bold, known satyr plays are marked by an asterisk. Alternative titles result from the concern of Alexandrian scholars to avoid confusion between two plays of the same name. For many of these plays only the bare title or perhaps a single line or two survives; sometimes lines survive which cannot be ascribed to any particular play (known as *adespota*, literally 'without an owner'). This subject can be pursued in the Loeb volume *Aeschylus II* by H.W. Smyth, with appendix and addendum by H. Lloyd-Jones.

Extant plays

472: ***Persians***
468-7: ***Seven Against Thebes***
467-56: ***Suppliants***
458: ***Oresteia trilogy: Agamemnon, Libation-Bearers, Eumenides***
    (late): ***Prometheus Bound*** (authorship disputed)

Attested tetralogies

472: *Phineus,* ***Persians,*** *Glaucus of Potniae, *Prometheus Fire-Kindler*
468-7: *Laius, Oedipus,* ***Seven Against Thebes,*** **Sphinx*: about Oedipus and Thebes
458: ***Agamemnon, Libation-Bearers, Eumenides,*** **Proteus*: about Orestes
(undated): *Edonian Women, Bassarids, Neaniskoi* (= *Young Men*), *Lycourgus*: about Lycurgus

Probable groups of plays (chronology uncertain)

Suppliants, *Egyptians, Danaids, *Amymone:* about the daughters of Danaus

136

*Psychagogoi (Spirit-Raisers), Ostologoi (Bone-Gatherers), Penelope, *Circe*: about Odysseus
Prometheus Bound, *Prometheus Set Free, Prometheus Fire-Bearer*: about Prometheus
Award of Arms, Thracian Women, Salaminians: about Ajax
Myrmidons, Nereids, Phrygians or *The Ransom of Hector*: about Achilles
*Argo, The Lemnians, Hypsipyle, *Cabeiri*: about Jason and the Argonauts
Eleusinians, Argives, Epigoni (= *Sons of the Seven*): about mythical Argive war with Thebes
Dictyoulkoi (Net-draggers), Polydectes, Daughters of Phorcis: about Danae and Perseus
Memnon, Psychostasia (Weighing of Souls)
Women of Perrhaebia, Ixion
Mysians, Telephus

Remaining titles

Five plays dealing with the Theban myth of Dionysus: *Semele* or *Water-Carriers, Nurses of Dionysus, Bacchae, Xantriae, Pentheus.*
The rest: *Aetnaeae* (= *Women of Etna*), *Alcmene, Atalanta, Athamas, Callisto, Carians* or *Europa, *Cercyon, *Cerukes* (= *Heralds* or *Messengers*), *Cretan Women* (in which the seer Polyidus restores Glaucus to life), *Cycnus, *Glaucus Pontius* (= *Glaucus of the Sea*), *Heliades* (about Phaethon), *Heraclidae* (= *Children of Heracles*), *Hiereiai* (= *Priestesses*), *Iphigeneia, Leon, Nemea, Niobe, *Oreithuia, Palamedes, Philoctetes, Propompoi,* (= *Processional Escorts*), *Sisyphus Drapetes* (= *Sisyphus the Runaway*), *Sisyphus Petrokulistes* (= *Sisyphus the Stone-Roller*) (perhaps two titles for the same play), *Thalamopoioi* (= *Makers of the Bridal Chambers* ?in which the Danaids murdered their husbands: if so, probably an alternative title for *Egyptians*), *Theoroi* (= *Spectators*) probably the same play as *Isthmiastae* (= *Spectators at the Isthmian Games*), *Toxotides* (= *The Archer-Maidens*) (about Actaeon).

Outline of *Agamemnon*

1-39 **Prologue**
The Watchman on the roof of the palace at Argos sets the scene. He has been waiting for news of Troy for nine years: now he sees the longed-for beacon-fire.

40-103 **Entry anapaests**
The chorus of Theban elders says it is ten years since Menelaus and Agamemnon set out for Troy; they themselves were already past fighting age then. The outcome of the expedition is unknown. Does Clytemnestra have information? She is silent.

104-257 **Parodos**
The chorus assume narrative authority. Ten years ago, as the expedition readied for departure from Aulis, a portent appeared of eagles devouring a hare, which the prophet Calchas interpreted as success for the army at Troy on the one hand, but the anger of Artemis on the other. In the following so-called 'Hymn to Zeus' (160-91) they ponder Zeus' harsh but educative intentions towards humans. The narrative continues. Artemis in her anger kept the winds contrary, preventing the expeditionary force from setting sail. Agamemnon made the decision to appease her by the sacrifice of his daughter Iphigeneia.

258-354 **First episode**
(Clytemnestra and chorus)
Clytemnestra informs the chorus of Troy's fall: in two speeches she describes first the movement of fire across a series of beacons linking Troy to Argos (the 'Beacon Speech'), then the contrasting fortunes of the winners and losers at Troy. She adds

that the Greeks must not offend the gods by desecrating religious spaces during their sack of Troy. At first sceptical, the chorus say they are now convinced by her narrative.

355-488 **First stasimon**
The chorus celebrates the victory. Zeus, god of hospitality, has now punished Paris' transgression when, as Menelaus' guest, he abducted Helen. Those who sin against what is sacred will be punished, and so will their kin. Wealth does not protect one from Justice. Paris' story exemplifies the pattern of crime and punishment.

When Helen left for Troy, prophets were inspired and Menelaus grieved. Because of Helen, many now grieve: War, like a money-changer, has taken living men and given them back as ashes in an urn. Relatives of the dead feel anger and the people are restless. Gods and Furies are fully aware of those who kill many, and they reverse the fortunes of those who prosper without justice. May they themselves never be involved in a sacking. But can the news – coming from a woman – really be true?

489-680 **Second episode**
(Herald and chorus, Clytemnestra)
Fresh from Troy, the Herald confirms the earlier news, unknowingly also confirming the fear that Agamemnon incurred impiety by destroying religious sites; in stichomythia the chorus attempts to convey the idea of danger in Argos, but the Herald blithely continues his narrative. Clytemnestra asserts that the Herald's news is confirmation of what she had said; soon Agamemnon himself will be back. The Herald tells them that Menelaus, however, has disappeared after a storm at sea.

681-781 **Second stasimon**
The chorus meditates on the appropriateness of Helen's name (the *hel-* prefix means something like 'deadly'). They compare her to a hand-reared lion cub – first charming, then murderous; her arrival in Troy as a bride was the arrival of a Fury. Too much prosperity (*koros*) leads to an act of arrogance (*hybris*)

and this in turn creates disaster (*atê*); the sequence is expressed genealogically, and it works genealogically down human generations. Justice steers everything to its appointed end.

782-809 **Entry anapaests**
The chorus heralds Agamemnon's triumphal entry on a chariot. In veiled terms they urge him to test the loyalty of his subjects.

810-974 **Third episode**
(Agamemnon and Clytemnestra: silent chorus and silent Cassandra)
Paying due respect to the gods, Agamemnon announces his success at Troy and, in response to the chorus, his readiness to deal with any dissidence in Argos. Clytemnestra describes her extreme nervous anxiety during his absence, and explains that their son Orestes has been taken for safe-keeping to Phocis. She is ecstatic to have her husband safely home. Will he step into the house on luxurious cloths? Agamemnon refuses on the grounds that it is arrogant and impious to trample on the wealth of the house, but is finally persuaded during a brief section of stichomythia in which his wife verbally outwits him. As he reluctantly walks up on the cloths to the central door of the stage building, Clytemnestra outrageously compares the riches of the palace to the inexhaustible wealth of the sea. In a series of extravagant phrases she compares the king to a vine-stock giving shade in summer, he is the sun's warmth after winter, the cool weather when grapes are pressed. He exits and she follows. Both are inside the stage building, Cassandra still on stage in the chariot (the second part of this episode is known as the carpet scene).

975-1034 **Third stasimon**
The chorus describe the pounding of their hearts. Why should they feel so disturbed since they have, after all, just witnessed Agamemnon's safe return? But only a hair's breadth separates a thing from its opposite, as is the case with health and sickness. Some dangers can be averted or modified, as cargo is

jettisoned from a ship to ensure its safety. But Death cannot be modified: the dead do not return to life. Inopportunely, their heart races ahead of anything their tongue can express.

1035-1330 Fourth episode
1035-71 (Clytemnestra, chorus, silent Cassandra)
Clytemnestra re-enters to persuade Cassandra inside too for a 'victory sacrifice'. The chorus tries to help, but Cassandra remains entirely mute and unmoving.

1072-1177 **Amoebean** (Cassandra and chorus).
Cassandra at last breaks her silence, singing of her ruin at the hand of Apollo and describing visionary fragments of the house's history: skewered babies eaten by a father, and now a hideous new crime: the bull gored in the bath. She foresees her own death. The chorus becomes increasingly agitated, but is unable to comprehend.

1178-1330 Cassandra now tries again in iambic trimeters. (The rest of this section consists of three *rhêseis* from Cassandra followed by generous sections of dialogue.) She describes a dancing troupe of Furies under the roof. She tells them that after she rejected Apollo's advances, he inflicted on her the punishment that she should prophesy but not be believed. Again she associates the past history of the house and its murdered children with the coming revenge-murder: no matter if the chorus cannot understand or believe her: it is going to happen anyway. The chorus remain unenlightened even when, in the second *rhêsis* (1214-41), Cassandra describes further visions. In despair she tears off her prophetic insignia. Composed again, she asserts that an avenger will come after her death: Orestes, whose father's murdered body will exert a force drawing him home to kill his mother. Three times Cassandra goes up to the entrance to the palace only to turn aside with more words: the chorus express profound sympathy for her coming death. Finally she enters the stage building.

1331-42 Choral anapaests
Left alone on stage, the chorus' apprehensions are growing: they speculate that real danger awaits their king.

1343-5 Agamemnon (offstage) cries out as he is struck down.

1346-71 In paired trimeters, individual members of the chorus react to the death cries with contradictory suggestions. No consensus is achieved before:

1372-1406 Clytemnestra enters from the palace door together with the corpses of Agamemnon and Cassandra. At last able to speak the truth freely, she declares that she exults in the murder of her husband.

1407-1576 Epirrhematic composition
(Clytemnestra, chorus)
The appalled chorus, in song, claims that the people will sentence Clytemnestra to banishment. In calmer iambic trimeters she counter-claims that Agamemnon, by sacrificing Iphigeneia, deserved to die. She has brought to fulfilment the *Dikê, Atê* and *Erinys* claimed by her daughter. And as long as Aegisthus 'lights the fire on her hearth' she is safe from punishment. She exults again over both bodies.

The chorus longs for death now their king is dead – killed by a woman, just as another woman, Helen, caused the death of so many. Clytemnestra, now chanting in anapaests, rejects this *'femme fatale'* rationalisation. The chorus' next suggestion is that the death was brought about by the *daimôn* of the house which attacks every generation. Clytemnestra assents to this line of approach, but this makes the chorus reflect on the role of Zeus in all this: he is the cause of all, and their lives are all pain. They grieve for their king.

Clytemnestra asserts her personal innocence of the murder: she was the mere embodiment of the *alastôr* (avenging spirit) set in motion by Agamemnon's father Atreus when he forced his brother Thyestes unwittingly to eat his own children and was cursed by him. The chorus rejects this: she is certainly guilty, and an *alastôr* may arise against her to avenge Agamemnon's murder (they are hinting at Orestes): but Clytemnestra again reminds them of Iphigeneia's claim. The chorus feels the house is collapsing under a rain of blood: *Dikê* is still sharpening her sword. And how will Agamemnon receive proper burial ritual from loving kin? Clytemnestra replies that his contact with kin will be with Iphigeneia in Hades.

The chorus sum up the debate. It is hard to decide between the claims and counter-claims, but Zeus' fixed law is that the perpetrator must suffer. The house is wedded to its ruin (*atê*). Clytemnestra, however, claims she will now be able to draw a line under the past and make the *daimôn* of the house depart.

1577-1648
(Clytemnestra, Aegisthus, chorus)

Aegisthus exults over Agamemnon's murder. He describes the quarrel between their two fathers, and the moment when Atreus falsely lured Thyestes back from exile and feasted him on the flesh of his own children. Himself the sole survivor, brought up in exile, he has returned and exacted *Dikê*. When the chorus claims the populace will punish him he turns on them with cruelty, reminding them of their physical powerlessness. He intends to 'break' the people to his will. The chorus taunts him with cowardice in leaving Clytemnestra to do his work for him; one day Orestes will kill them both.

1649-end **Exodos**
In trochaic tetrameters Aegisthus and the chorus draw their swords but Clytemnestra intervenes. Still uttering threats and insults, the chorus departs and Clytemnestra and Aegisthus enter the house to assume control.

Select Bibliography

Abbreviations

AJPh = *American Journal of Philology*
AS = *Agamemnon Staged: Proceedings of the Agamemnon Conference 2001* (Oxford, 2005)
BICS = *Bulletin of the Institute of Classical Studies*
CCGT = P.E. Easterling (ed.), *The Cambridge Companion to Greek Tragedy* (Cambridge, 1997)
CPh = *Classical Philology*
CQ = *Classical Quarterly*
G&R = *Greece and Rome*
HSCPh = *Harvard Studies in Classical Philology*
ICS = *Institute of Classical Studies*
JHS = *Journal of Hellenic Studies*
PCPhS = *Proceedings of the Cambridge Philological Society*
TAPhA = *Transactions of the American Philological Association*

Greek texts with English commentaries

Denniston, J.D. and Page, D., *Aeschylus Agamemnon*, edited with commentary (Oxford, 1957)
Fraenkel, E., *Aeschylus Agamemnon*, edited with translation and commentary, 3 vols (Oxford, 1950)

Translations

Collard, C., *Aeschylus, Oresteia* (Oxford, 2002), accurate with helpful introduction
Ewans, M., *Aischylos, The Oresteia* (London, 1995), written for performance
De May, P., *Aeschylus, Agamemnon* (Cambridge, 2003), accurate, with simple running critique
Fagles, R., *Aeschylus, The Oresteia* (New York, 1966), current Black Penguin Classic; free

144

Harrison, T., *The Oresteia* (London, 1982), free
Hughes, T., *The Oresteia* (London, 1999), free
Lloyd-Jones, H., *Agamemnon by Aeschylus,* trans. with commentary, Prentice-Hall Greek Drama series (New Jersey, 1970; reprinted in *Aeschylus Oresteia,* London and Dallas, 1979)
Meineck, P., *Aeschylus, Oresteia* with introduction by Helene Foley (Indianapolis, 1998), written for performance
Shapiro, A. and Burian, P., *Aeschylus, The Oresteia* (Oxford, 2003), thoughtful translation with excellent introduction by Burian, very useful full notes and glossary
Smyth, H.W., *Aeschylus, Agamemnon, Libation-Bearers, Eumenides, Fragments,* with appendix and addendum by Hugh Lloyd-Jones, 1957 (Cambridge, Mass. and London 1929), close Loeb parallel text edition

Books and articles

Beacham, R.C., *The Roman Theatre and its Audience* (London, 1991)
Boyle, A.J., *Tragic Seneca: An Essay in the Theatrical Tradition* (London and New York, 1997)
Burian, P., 'Myth into *Muthos*: The Shaping of Tragic Plot', *CCGT,* pp. 178-208
Buxton, R.G.A., *The Complete World of Greek Mythology* (London, 2004)
―――― *Persuasion in Greek Tragedy: A Study of Peitho* (Cambridge, 1982)
Carey, C., *Democracy in Classical Athens* (London, 2000)
Cartledge, P., ' "Deep Plays": Theatre as Process in Greek Civic Life', *CCGT,* pp. 3-35
Coffey, M., 'Seneca and His Tragedies', *Proceedings of the African Classical Association* vol. 3 (1960), p. 16
Cohen, D., 'The Theodicy of Aeschylus: Justice and Tyranny in the *Oresteia', G&R* (1986), repr. in I. McAuslan and P. Walcot (eds), *Greek Tragedy* (Oxford, 1993)
Davies, M., *The Epic Cycle* (Bristol, 1989)
Dawe, R.D., 'Inconsistency of Plot and Character in Aeschylus', *PCPhS* 189 n.s. 9 (1963), pp. 21-62
Earp, F.R., *The Style of Aeschylus* (Cambridge, 1948)
Easterling, P.E., 'Agamemnon for the Ancients', *AS,* ch. 1
―――― (ed.), *The Cambridge Companion to Greek Tragedy* (Cambridge, 1997)
―――― 'Form and Performance', *CCGT,* pp. 151-77
―――― 'A Show for Dionysus', *CCGT,* pp. 36-68
―――― 'Constructing Character in Greek Tragedy', pp. 83-99 in C. Pelling (ed.), *Characterization and Individuality in Greek Literature* (Oxford, 1990)

——— 'Women in Tragic Space', *BICS* 34 (1987), pp. 15-26

——— 'Presentation of Character in Aeschylus', *G&R* 20 (1973), pp. 3-19

Ewbank, I-S., 'Striking too Short at Greeks', *AS*, ch. 3

Ferrari, G., 'Figures in the Text: Metaphors and Riddles in the *Agamemnon*', *CPh* 92 (1997), pp. 1-45

Foley, H.P., *Female Acts in Greek Tragedy* (New Jersey and Oxford), 2001

——— 'The Conception of Women in Greek Drama', in H.P. Foley (ed.), *Reflections of Women in Antiquity* (New York, 1981), pp. 127-68

Gagarin, M., *Aeschylean Drama* (Berkeley, Los Angeles and London, 1976)

Gantz, T.N., 'The Fires of the *Oresteia*', *JHS* (1977), pp. 28-38

Garvie, A.F., 'Aeschylus' Simple Plots', in R.D. Dawe, J. Diggle and P.E. Easterling (eds), *Dionysiaca: Nine Studies by Former Pupils Presented to Sir Denys Page on his Seventieth Birthday* (Cambridge, 1978), pp. 63-86

Gentili, B., *Theatrical Performances in the Ancient World: Hellenistic and Early Roman Theatre* (Amsterdam, 1979)

Goldhill, S., *The Oresteia*, Landmarks of World Literature series (Cambridge, 1992; 2nd edn 2004)

——— 'The Language of Tragedy: Rhetoric and Communication', *CCGT*, pp. 127-50

——— 'The Great Dionysia and Civic Ideology' in J.J. Winkler and F. Zeitlin (eds), *Nothing To Do With Dionysus: Athenian Drama in its Social Context* (Princeton, 1990)

——— *Reading Greek Tragedy* (Cambridge, 1986)

——— *Language, Sexuality, Narrative: The Oresteia* (Cambridge 1984)

Gould, J., 'Dramatic Character and "Human Intelligibility" in Greek tragedy', *PCPhS* 14, pp. 43-67, repr. in *Myth, Ritual Memory and Exchange* (Oxford, 2001)

Goward, B., *Telling Tragedy: Narrative Technique in Aeschylus, Sophocles and Euripides* (London, 1999)

Hall, E., 'Clytemnestra versus her Senecan Tradition', *AS*, ch. 4

——— 'Eating Children is Bad for You: The Offspring of the Past in Aeschylus' *Agamemnon*', in D. Stuttard and T. Shasha (eds), *Essays on Agamemnon* (Brighton, 2002), pp. 11-26

——— 'The Sociology of Athenian Tragedy', *CCGT*, pp. 93-126

Hardwick, L., *Reception Studies*, *G&R* New Surveys in the Classics no. 33 (Oxford, 2003)

Helm, J.J., 'Aeschylus and the Genealogy of Morals', *TAPhA* 134 (2004), pp. 23-54

Henry, D. and Walker, B., 'Seneca and the *Agamemnon*: Some Thoughts on Tragic Doom', *CPh* 58 (1963), pp. 1-10

Herington, C.J., *Aeschylus* (New Haven and London, 1986)

—— *Poetry into Drama: Early Tragedy and the Greek Poetic Tradition*, Sather Classical Lectures 49 (California and London, 1985)

—— 'Senecan Tragedy', *Arion* 5 (1966), pp. 422-71

—— 'Aeschylus: The Last Phase', *Arion* IV.3 (1965), pp. 367-403, repr. in E. Segal (ed.), *Oxford Readings in Greek Tragedy* (Oxford, 1983)

Jenkins, I., 'The Ambiguity of Greek Textiles', *Arethusa* 18.2 (Fall 1985)

Knox, B., 'Aeschylus and the Third Actor', *AJPh* 93.1 (1972), repr. in B. Knox, *Word in Action* (Baltimore, 1979)

—— 'The Lion in the House', *CPh* 47 (1952), repr. in B. Knox, *Word in Action* (Baltimore, 1979)

Lebeck, A., *The Oresteia: A Study in Language and Structure* (Cambridge Mass., 1971)

Lesky, A., 'Decision and Responsibility in the Tragedy of Aeschylus', *JHS* 86 (1966), pp. 78-86, repr. in E. Segal (ed.), *Oxford Readings in Greek Tragedy* (Oxford 1982)

Lloyd, M., *The Agon in Euripides* (Oxford, 1992)

Lloyd-Jones, H., *The Justice of Zeus*, Sather Classical Lectures 41 (Los Angeles and London, 1971; 2nd edition 1983)

—— 'The Guilt of Agamemnon', *CQ* 12 (1962), pp. 187-99, repr. with minor revisions in E. Segal (ed.), *Oxford Readings in Greek Tragedy* (Oxford, 1982)

—— *Agamemnon by Aeschylus,* trans. with commentary, Prentice-Hall Greek Drama series (New Jersey, 1970), repr. in *Aeschylus Oresteia* (London and Dallas, 1979)

Lowe, N.J., *The Classical Plot and the Invention of Classical Narrative* (Cambridge, 2000)

Macintosh, F. (ed.), *Agamemnon Staged: Proceedings of the Agamemnon Conference 2001* (Oxford, 2005)

March, J.R., 'The Creative Poet', *ICS* suppl. 49 (1987), pp. 79-118

Michelakis, P., 'Agamemnons in Performance', *AS*, Introduction

Miller, F.J., *Seneca's Tragedies I, II,* Loeb Classical Library (London and New York, 1917)

Miola, R.S., *Shakespeare and Classical Tragedy: The Influence of Seneca* (Oxford, 1992)

Nussbaum, M.C., *The Fragility of Goodness: Luck and Ethics in Greek Tragedy and Philosophy* (Cambridge, 1986; rev. edn 2001)

Peradotto, J.J., 'Some Patterns of Nature Imagery in the *Oresteia*', *AJPh* 85 (1964), pp. 379-93

Peradotto, J.J., 'The Omen of the Eagles', *Phoenix* 23 (1969), pp. 237-43

Pickard-Cambridge, A., *The Dramatic Festivals of Athens,* 2nd edn revised by J. Gould and Lewis (Oxford, 1988)

Podlecki, A.J., *The Political Background of Aeschylean Tragedy* (Ann Arbor, 1966; 2nd edn London, 1999), pp. 63-100

Prince, G., *Dictionary of Narratology* (Nebraska, 1987)

Rabinowitz, P., 'What's Hecuba to Us? The Audience's Experience of Literary Borrowings', in S.R. Suleiman and I. Crosman (eds), *The Reader in the Text* (Princeton, 1980), pp. 241-63

—— 'Truth in Fiction: A Re-examination of Audiences', *Critical Inquiry* 4 (1977), pp. 121-42

Rehm R., *The Play of Space* (New Jersey, 2002), p. 76ff.

—— *Greek Tragic Theatre* (London and New York, 1992)

Rimmon-Kenan, R., *Narrative Fiction: Contemporary Poetics* (London and New York, 1983)

Roberts, D.H., *Apollo and his Oracle in the Oresteia* (Gottingen, 1984)

Robinson, E.W., *Ancient Greek Democracy: Readings and Sources* (Oxford, 2004)

Rosenmeyer, T.G., *The Art of Aeschylus* (Los Angeles and London, 1982)

Silk, M.S. (ed.), *Tragedy and the Tragic: Greek Theatre and Beyond* (Oxford, 1996)

Solmsen, F., *Hesiod and Aeschylus,* Cornell Studies in Classical Philology vol. 30 (New York, 1949)

Sommerstein, A.H., *Aeschylean Tragedy* (Bari, 1996)

Stanford, W.B., *Aeschylus in his Style* (Dublin, 1942)

Taplin, O., *Greek Tragedy in Action* (Oxford, 1978)

—— *The Stagecraft of Aeschylus: The Dramatic Use of Exits and Entrances in Greek Tragedy* (Oxford, 1977)

Tarrant, R.J., 'Senecan Drama and its Antecedents', *HSCPh* 82 (1978), pp. 213-64

—— *Seneca Agamemnon,* edited with a commentary (Cambridge, 1976)

Vidal-Nacquet, P., 'Hunting and Sacrifice in Aeschylus' *Oresteia'*, in J-P. Vernant and P. Vidal-Nacquet, *Tragedy and Myth in Ancient Greece* (Brighton and New Jersey, 1981), ch. 7; first published in France as *Mythe et Tragedie en Grece Ancienne* (Paris, 1972)

Webster, T.B.L., 'Some Psychological Terms in Greek Tragedy', *JHS* 77 (1957), 149-54

Wiles, D., *Tragedy in Athens: Performance Space and Theatrical Meaning* (Cambridge, 1997)

Winnington-Ingram, R.P., *Studies in Aeschylus* (Cambridge, 1983)

Wrigley, A., '*Agamemnons* on the Database', *AS*, ch. 19

Zeitlin, F.I., 'The Motif of the Corrupted Sacrifice in Aeschylus' *Oresteia*', *TAPhA* 96 (1965), 463-508, repr. in Zeitlin, *Playing the Other* (Chicago, 1996)

—— 'Postscript to Sacrificial Imagery in the *Oresteia*', *TAPhA* 96 (1965), pp. 463-508

Chronology

Listed here are some key productions, adaptations and re-workings of *Agamemnon* (sometimes Senecan rather than Aeschylean) in original and vernacular translation. No school or student production has been included, nor any of the large number of operatic treatments; the list is biased towards English language versions. These entries derive from the APGRD (Archive of Performances of Greek and Roman Drama) database, compiled by Amanda Wrigley.

BC
458: *Oresteia* by Aeschylus, Athens
452-451: *Agamemnon* by Ion of Chios, Athens (lost)
240-207: *Aegisthus* by Livius Andronicus, Rome (lost)
140-86: *Clytemnestra* by Lucius Accius, Rome (lost)
55: Accius' *Clytemnestra* revived for gala opening of Pompey's Theatre, Rome

AD
49-65: *Agamemnon* by Seneca, Rome
1584: *Agamemnon and Ulysses*, Greenwich, London (lost)
1599: *Agamemnon* adapted by Henry Chettle and Thomas Dekker, Elizabeth Rose Theatre, London
c. **1609-13:** *The Iron Age,* including an adaptation of *Agamemnon* as part of a series of four *Ages*, by Thomas Heywood; Red Bull, London
c. **1609-13:** *The Tragedie of Orestes*, original play in English by Thomas Goffe based on Eur. *Orestes,* Sen. *Agamemnon* and *Thyestes,* Shakespeare *Hamlet* and Soph. *Electra*; Christ Church, Oxford
c. **1619-22:** *The True Tragedie of Herod and Antipater* by Gervase Markham and William Sampson; this includes a 'Dumbe Shewe' of the murder in *Agamemnon*; Red Bull, London
1738: *Agamemnon,* adapted from Seneca and Aeschylus by James Thomson, Drury Lane, London

Chronology

1794: *Clytemnestre*, cantata for solo voice by Cherubini, France
1797: *Agamemnon* adapted by 'Citizen' Lemercier from Seneca and Agamemnon, Théâtre de la République, Paris
1816: *Agamemnon* read by Napoleon to companions on Saint Helena
1842: *Agamennone* adapted by Alfieri, Teatro Re, Milan
1868: *Agamemnon and Cassandra; or, The Prophet and Loss of Troy!*, burlesque by Robert Reece, Liverpool, Dublin and Portsmouth
1873: *Les Erinnyes,* adaptation of *Agamemnon* and *Libation-Bearers* by Leconte de Lisle; revivals had music by Massenet. France
1880: May: *Agamemnon*, translated by L. Campbell, produced by Fleeming Jenkin in his private theatre, Edinburgh
1880: June: *Agamemnon* in original Greek, produced by F. Benson at Balliol, Oxford and then on tour
1885: *The Orestean Trilogy of Aeschylus* in translation, produced in Cambridge by Benson and then on tour
1886: *The Story of Orestes* (abridged version of *Oresteia*), translated and directed by G.C.W. Warr, Piccadilly, London
1904: *The Orestean Trilogy of Aeschylus* performed in London and on tour
1931: Premiere of Eugene O'Neill's *Mourning Becomes Electra,* an adaptation of the *Oresteia,* Guild Theatre, New York
1936: Louis MacNeice's translation of *Agamemnon,* directed by Rupert Doone with music by Benjamin Britten, performed Westminster Theatre, London
1937: *Mourning Becomes Electra* performed in London
1946: Louis MacNeice's *Agamemnon* performed on BBC radio, directed by Val Gielgud
1947: Film of *Mourning Becomes Electra*, directed by Dudley Nichols, USA
1955: *Mourning Becomes Electra*, directed by Peter Hall, Arts Theatre, London
1957: *Agamemnon,* translated by Richmond Lattimore, directed by Wayne Richardson, Theater Marquee, New York
1958: *Clytemnestra,* three-act dance treatment of *Oresteia,* choreographed by Martha Graham, Adelphi Theatre, New York; frequently revived and on tour in Europe
1962: *Song of a Goat,* version of *Agamemnon* by J.P. Clark, directed by Wole Soyinka, Mbari Centre, Ibadan, Nigeria. Later performed in London. New production, Lagos, 1991
1973: *Agamemnon Part 1,* adapted and directed by Steven Berkoff, Round House, London and again in 1976
1973: *The Orphan* by D. Rabe, drawing on *Oresteia* and Eur. *Iphigeneia in Aulis,* directed by Jeff Bleckner, New York; twice revived in 1974

Chronology

1973: *Appunti per un'Orestiade Africana*; film directed by P.P. Pasolini, shown first in Venice and then USA

1979: *The Serpent Son,* adapted by F. Raphael and K. McLeish, broadcast in three parts on BBC 2 television; new production in Sheffield, 1991

1980: *Agamemnon,* part of *The Greeks,* ten Greek tragedies adapted by John Barton and Kenneth Cavander, directed by Barton; Aldwych Theatre, London. Tours in USA in 1981, 1982, 1985 and 1986; many revivals

1980: *Die Orestie,* translated and directed by Peter Stein; Berlin, then Paris and Ostia

1981: *Oresteia,* translated by Tony Harrison, directed by Peter Hall with music by Harrison Birtwhistle, Olivier Theatre, London and on tour in Epidauros. Broadcast on Channel 4 TV, 1983

1987: *Oresteia,* translated by P.P. Pasolini, directed by L. Salveti, Vicenza

1990: *Les Atrides,* adaptation of the *Oresteia* preceded by Eur. *Iphigeneia in Aulis.* Translated by Jean Bollack, Ariane Mnouchkine, Helene Cixous; directed by Mnouchkine. The Theatre du Soleil performed in Paris and then toured internationally until 1993

1992: *The Gift of the Gorgon,* loose adaptation of *Agamemnon* by Peter Shaffer, directed by Peter Hall, Pit Theatre, London, then Wyndham's

1992: *The Clytemnestra Project:* translations of *Iphigeneia in Aulis, Agamemnon* and *Electra,* directed by G. Wright, Guthrie Theater, Minneapolis; new productions in South Dakota and Los Angeles 1991, Massachusetts and Los Angeles 2001 and 2003

1993: *Klytemnestra's Bairns,* adaptation of *Oresteia* by Bill Dunlop, directed by Toby Gough, Edinburgh

1994: Peter Stein's 1980 production of *Oresteia* revived with changes and translated by Boris Shekassiouk for Moscow, then on tour

1996: *L'Orestie,* adapted and directed by Silviu Purcarete, Limoges, France. Revised production given at National Theatre of Craiova, Romania, and on tour in Britain, 1998

1999: *The Oresteia: Part One The Home Guard, Part Two Daughters of Darkness,* translated by Ted Hughes, directed by Katie Mitchell, Cottesloe Theatre, London

2002: *Ariel,* adapted from *Iphigeneia in Aulis* and the *Oresteia* by Marina Carr, directed by Conall Morrison, Abbey Theatre, London

2003: *Mourning Becomes Electra,* directed by Howard Davies, Lyttleton Theatre, London

Glossary

In the theatre

aulêtês: musician with a double pipe accompanying the sung parts of the play

deuteragonist: the second actor

ekkyklêma: flat cart, wheeled out from the *skênê* to show a tableau from inside

eisodos: wide entrance into the *orchêstra*, one on each side of the *skênê*

kôphon prosôpon: lit. 'empty mask', a non-speaking actor

koryphaios: the chorus-leader

mêchanê: a crane positioned behind the *skênê,* originally used for divine epiphanies

orchêstra: round central area of the theatre

parodos: alternative name for *eisodos*

protagonist: the first actor

skênê: the stage building at the back of the *orchêstra*

tritagonist: the third actor

In the text

agôn: a scene of dispute between two characters

amoebaean: matching groups of sung verse assigned alternately to two characters

anapaest: simple, heavily rhythmic metre suitable for walking to, and so often used while characters process into or out of the *orchêstra*

antilabê: division of a line of verse between two speakers

distichomythia: dialogue between two characters in double alternating verses (i.e. two each)

epeisodion or **episode**: the portions of dialogue between two choral odes

epirrhematic composition: a dialogue in which only one participant sings

exodos: the closing section of the play leading to the exit of the chorus

kommos: lament sung alternately by one or more characters and the chorus

Glossary

parodos: the chorus' first entry-song
prologue: the material of the play preceding the chorus' first entry
rhêsis: a continuous speech by one character
stichomythia: dialogue between two characters in single alternating
    lines of verse (i.e. one each)
stasimon: choral song between episodes

Index

Aegisthus, 7, 23, 35, 42, 44, 54, 57, 58, 80, 88, 107, 109, 115, 117, 122f.

Aeschylus: life, 10f.; epitaph, 12; output, 12, 16f., 136-7

Agamemnon, king of Argos, 7, 9, 10, 23; chariot entry and barefoot exit, 32f.; death cries, 38, 39; earlier treatments, 43-7; 52, 55, 58; his dilemma, 62f.; 66, 67, 70, 79, 85; reception of murder, 107, 115

Agamemnon: *passim*; ethical concerns, 14, 62-3; legal aspects, 14, 92-3; story of, 15; formal structure and outline of, 22f., 138f.; assignation of roles, 23; symbolic dimensions of, 29f.; Beacon Speech, 31, 64, 98; chariot entry, 27, 32, 120; lure-murder, 33; carpet-scene, 33f., 56, 89, 120, 128; *exodos*, 42; scene-shape, 50; causality, 54f.; entry-anapaests and *parodos*, 60f., 98f.; stichomythia (931-43), 66, 95; characters in, 80f.; paired characters, 84; gender in, 85; third *stasimon* (975f.), 95-6; reception of, 109f.; Seneca's remake, 115f.; compared with *Hamlet*, 128f.

alastôr (the driver-astray or avenging spirit), 42, 57, 73, 76

APGRD, *see* Archive of Performances of Greek and Roman Drama

Apollo, 37, 38, 53, 56, 59, 70, 85, 95, 102

Archive of Performances of Greek and Roman Drama, 110

Aristophanes, 26, 27, 37, 102-3, 112

Aristotle, 19, 81, 93

Artemis, 46, 54, 55, 62, 70, 76, 85, 98, 99

atê (disaster, ruin), 32, 53, 73-5, 95

Athens, 10, 11, 13-14, 85-7, 92

Atridae (Agamemnon and Menelaus, the sons of Atreus), 7, 84-5, 101-2

audience, 15; authorial and narrative, 48f.

banquets and plays-within-plays, 7, 44, 126f.

Burian, P., 79

Calchas, 43, 55, 57, 61, 62, 64, 67, 70, 98-100, 101

Cassandra, 10, 23, 28, 34, 36; exit, 38-9; 41, 43, 46, 49, 52f., 56-8; 67, 70, 80, 85, 87-9; denied *peithô*, 97; final lines, 103; 107, 109, 111, 114, 116, 118f.

causality, problems of, 54f.
Choephoroe, see Libation-Bearers
choral lyric, 10; as origin of
tragedy, 18f.; typical nature
and capacities of, 19, 22
chorus of *Agamemnon: passim*,
14, 20; reaction to carpet, 35;
to death cries, 39-40; narrative
voice in opening anapaests and
parodos, 59f.; as repositories of
traditional wisdom, 75f.;
inability to grasp the truth,
95f., 116
chronology of productions, 150
Clytemnestra: *passim*, 7, 9, 23,
26; problematic entries and
exits, 29-30; control of
threshold, 32, 33, 35; in
carpet-scene, 33f.; with
Cassandra, 36, 38-9, 52-3; in
tableau, 41; earlier
Clytemnestras, 43-7; 49, 52,
55-8; narrative voice, 63f.; 70,
80; in Gould's reading, 83f.;
paired with Helen, 84; as
murderess, 88f.; 94-5, 100-1,
103, 105-7; in reception, 110f.
Cypria, 45, 46

daimôn, 42, 55, 57, 73, 76, 85;
daimones, 73f., 93, 104
defamiliarisation, 49
dêmos and compounds, 102
Denniston, J.D. and Page, D., 30,
65, 80, 95-6, 99
Dikê or *Dika, see* Justice
discrepant awareness, 49f., 128
dithyramb, 14

Easterling, P.E., 81, 82
eisodos, 26f.
ekkyklêma, 26f., 41

Eliot, T.S., 117
English Renaissance revenge
dramas, 124f.
Ephialtes, 12
Epic Cycle, 45, 118
epic poetry, 10, 20f.; Aeschylus'
transformation of, 98f.
Erinyes, see Furies
Eumenides, 9,12, 27, 41, 88, 92,
111
Euripides, 27, 35, 40, 46, 47, 51,
54, 63, 76, 81, 109, 112, 115,
116, 118-22
Ewbank, I.-S., 112

fallax fortuna, 116, 120, 129
focalisation, 57-8
Fraenkel, E., 23 n.19, 64, 80
Furies, 9, 10, 27, 30, 39, 41, 50,
53, 56, 67, 78, 96, 106, 107

gender, 65, 85f.
gods, 10, 30-2, 69f.
Goldhill, S., 60, 79, 82, 88, 92
Gould, J., 82
Great Dionysia, 11, 13f.

Hamlet, 111, 126f.
hapax legomena, 100f.
Helen, 7, 10, 31, 32, 45, 52, 57, 67,
76, 79, 84, 85, 89, 94, 100-2
Herald, 23, 27, 31, 32, 51, 52, 56.
58, 64, 65, 70, 94, 118f.
Hesiod, 72f., 76, 84
Homer, 15, 21f., 57, 72, 78; *Iliad*,
21, 22, 43, 74, 81; *Odyssey*,
44f., 51, 98
House of Atreus, 7, 30, 38f., 41,
42, 45, 47, 53, 56, 66-7, 72, 76,
80
human characters, 80f.
hybris, 56, 72, 73, 74-5

Index

Hymn to Zeus, 54, 61, 77, 78

imagery, 91, 103f.; 'trampling', 105; 'the net', 106f.
Iphigeneia, 34, 41, 46, 54-5, 62f., 65, 67, 70, 80, 85, 99, 100-1, 107, 109

Jacobson, R., 97, 100
Justice (*Dikê* or *Dika*), 14, 50, 71f., 75, 77f., 105, 107

Knox, B., 37, 98 n.9, 104
kôphon prosôpon, 27, 36f., 122
koryphaios, 19, 20, 23, 59

language, 82f., 91f.; choral and civic, 92f.; powers and dangers of, 93f.; proper name puns, 93f.; *euphêmia, dysphêmia* and silence, 30, 94; persuasion and lack of it, 95-7
Leavis, F.R., 105, 106
Lebeck, A., 91, 99, 102
Libation-Bearers, 9, 28, 35, 37, 40, 41, 51, 53, 111
libera mors, 119
liturgy, 13 n.7
Lloyd-Jones, H., 71 nn.1&2, 78
lure-murders, 33f.

mêchanê, 27
Menelaus, 10, 31, 52, 56, 64, 85, 101
metre, 23 n.21
Miola, R.S., 129f.
myth, 19, 20f., earlier myths of Agamemnon's homecoming, 43f.

narrative technique, 43f.; 'story' and 'plot' contrasted, 49f.;

narrative voice, 57f.; of chorus, 59f.; of Clytemnestra, 63f.; embedded voices, 67f.
Nero, 113-14, 124
net, 46, 106f.
nostos (return home), 9, 51, 52-3, 59
Nussbaum, M., 14, 63

offstage cries, 39f.
oikos (house, family), 10, 26, 38f., 86
orchêstra, 24f.
Oresteia, outline of, 9-10,12, 50, 72, 78, 87, 91, 116
Orestes, 10, 35, 37, 41, 42, 43, 44, 50, 57, 66, 76, 111, 121-2

pathei mathos (learning through suffering), 61-2, 69-70, 71, 77, 80
Panatheneia, 10, 11
Pandora, 84
Paris, 7, 31, 52, 76, 105, 106
Peisistratos, 10, 11, 85
Peithô (Persuasion), 73, 75, 95, 97, 104
Pericles, 12, 13, 85
Persians, 12, 17, 25, 33, 51, 100
Pickard-Cambridge, A., 23
Pindar, 12, 18, 46
polis (community, society, city), 10, 14, 79
portent of eagles, 55, 98f.
Prometheus Bound, 12, 16, 17, 77

Rabinowitz, P., 48
reception of *Agamemnon*, 109f.
religion, 70f.
revenge, 124f.; its transformation in *Hamlet*, 129f.
Russian Formalists, 49

sacrilege, 55f.
satyr plays, 10, 14
Sauravius, 111
Seneca, 111, 114-15, 124, 129f.
Seneca's *Agamemnon*, 115-23, 125-7
Seven Against Thebes, 12, 25
Shakespeare, 16, 124, 126f.
silence, 30, 36-7, 37, 93-4
skênê: development of, 24f.; use in *Ag.*, 29f., 38, 39
Slater, P.E., 87
Solon, 17, 74
Sophocles,, 12, 19, 20, 26, 28, 35, 37, 40, 41, 46, 51, 81, 109, 118, 123
Stesichorus, 18, 46
style, 97f.; transformation of traditional features, 98-9; violence of, 97f.; compound words and coinages, 98f.; metaphor and ambiguity, 98f., 102; catachresis, 100; personification, 104; *see also* imagery; language.
suasoria, 113, 114

Suppliants, 12, 17, 25, 77
suspense, 15, 47f., 59

tableaux and mirror tableaux, 41
Taplin, O., 29, 30, 32
Tarrant, R.J., 111, 114
tetralogies, 16-17, 136-7
text, problems of, 16, 28
theatre: diagram of, 25; symbolic space, 24-7, 33f., 89-90
Thyestes, 7, 42, 44, 53, 54, 109, 115, 122, 126
time, 51f.
tragedy: as poetry, 17-18; origins, 18f.; structure of, 22-3
trampling, 34, 105f.

Vergil, 118, 120

Watchman, 23, 29, 38, 50, 52, 69, 71, 91, 93, 101
Winnington-Ingram, R.P., 78
women, role of, 15, 85f.

Zeus, 31, 45, 59-62, 69ff., 94, 99, 106-7, 115-16